KEEPING HER TRUST

SERENITY SPRINGS BOOK 5

DAWN SULLIVAN

Published by Dawn Sullivan
Cover Design: Dana Leah with Designs by Dana
Photographer: Bobby Lynn with Stonetown Arts, LLC
Model: Dawn D'Argenio
Edited by: Jamie White and CP Bialois
Copyright 2019 © Author Dawn Sullivan
Language: English

To my readers. Thank you so much for all of your support. It makes my heart happy.

$\mathcal{N}$athan Brentworth raked a hand through his thick, jet-black hair, sending a cocky smile toward the willowy brunette leaning against the bar next to him. She was gorgeous, with sultry brown eyes that pulled a man in, flawless skin he knew would be soft if he trailed his fingers over it, and waves of long, silky hair that hung in loose ringlets down her back, just touching her waist. She was a woman who could entrap you with a look, and have you hanging onto her every word within minutes.

Nodding to the bartender, he took the glass of whiskey, threw some cash down, and turned to face the stage, faking interest in the band that was playing. He didn't even have to wait a full minute before she made her move.

"Hello," she said in a low, husky voice, leaning in close and laying a hand lightly on his shoulder as she pressed her full breasts against his arm. "I haven't seen you here before."

There were so many things Nathan wanted to say at that moment, and only years of being on the job stopped him. He was fucking tired of this crap. He used to love going undercover, becoming a new person with a different alias every few months, infiltrating places no one else could and bringing down the bad guys. He was good at what he did, the best the Federal Bureau of Investigation had ever seen, and he had become a legend in his field. He used to think that was all that mattered. He'd lived for the job, and was prepared to die for the job… until he met her. The one woman who managed to capture his attention when no one else had.

Glancing over at the brunette, Nathan fought back the urge to turn and walk out of the bar. Unfortunately, that wasn't an option. Her dark red lips turned up in a smile, her brown eyes roaming over his body with interest. The vision in red had absolutely nothing on the woman he couldn't seem to stop thinking about. When she looked at him expectantly, waiting for him to respond, he shrugged, "Probably because I've never been here before."

No, he'd never been inside the dimly lit lounge, but he had been to several places just like it. Doing the same thing he was doing now. Getting close to the one person who could get him access to what he really wanted: a meeting with the head of the biggest drug cartel in the eastern states. Nathan had been stalking the cartel for several weeks, looking for his chance. Now, he finally had it.

"Why not?" Pricilla Braxton purred, sliding in closer and slipping an arm around his waist.

Making a show of taking a drink of the whiskey, even though not one drop actually went down his throat, Nathan grinned. "Just got into town, sweetheart."

Pricilla placed a palm on his chest, moving it up to curl

her fingers around the back of his neck. "Lucky me," she breathed in his ear.

"Pricilla, what the hell is going on here?" A man appeared in front of them, glaring at Pricilla. Nathan knew who he was. Her brother's bodyguard, and also her lover when she wanted him to be.

Nathan set his glass of whiskey on the bar behind him and slid an arm around her waist, glancing down at her. "Pricilla?" When she licked her lips and nodded, moving in even closer, he lowered his head and said, "I like it."

It was a lie. He hated it, and didn't think much more of her. He'd done his homework on the entire Braxton family. There wasn't an angel in the bunch. Not even the mother. She was even more vicious than her son, if that was possible.

"Good." Her eyes skated away from his to land on her brother's bodyguard. "Leave us, Javier. This gentleman and I have much to talk about."

Javier glared at Nathan, his eyes full of anger and instant hatred. "No, Pricilla, you don't have a fucking thing to talk about. Your brother wants to see you. Now."

Pricilla's eyes turned hard, her lips firming into a thin line. "Bernardo does not tell me what to do, Javier, and neither do you. I will be over when I am ready, and not before."

Javier moved closer, growling menacingly, "You will come now, Pricilla, or I am under orders to make you come. You choose. The easy way...or my way?"

When Javier reached for her, Nathan slid Pricilla behind him, stepping between her and the bodyguard. Placing his hands lightly on his hips, he made it a point to subtly slide his suit jacket open, showing the other man he was packing heat. "I suggest you keep your hands off the lady." *Lady hell,* he thought, suppressing a shudder. The woman was a fucking viper, but he had a part to play if he wanted a chance to take down her brother.

Javier stepped close enough that their chests brushed together, his dark brown eyes blazing with fury as he growled, "I don't know who you think you are messing with family business, but I suggest *you* back the fuck off unless you want to end up in a body bag."

"Javier!" Pricilla snapped, moving quickly around Nathan and stomping her foot. "Stop this! You can't threaten every single man I talk to!"

"Wanna bet?"

"What's going on here, little sister?"

Nathan didn't take his gaze from the man in front of him, not letting his guard down for a second. Javier was a vicious fighter, especially when it involved Pricilla.

"Dammit, Bernardo! All I was doing was talking to this nice gentleman. Then, your freaking pitbull had to step in."

"Nice gentleman? Do you even know his name, Pricilla?" There was laughter in Bernardo Braxton's voice when he replied, but Nathan wasn't deceived. The man was a snake, pure and simple. Just like his viper of a sister. He would treat you as if you were his best friend one minute, and put a hit out on you the next.

"No, I hadn't gotten that far, yet," Pricilla admitted, stomping her foot again. "Tell him to back off, Bernardo. I mean it!"

There was a moment of silence, then, "Javier, why don't you buy our new friend a drink?" When Javier didn't move, Bernardo's voice became hard as steel. "Now."

Leaning in close, Javier snarled, "You lay one hand on what is mine, I will break every bone in your body."

Nathan didn't bother to respond. He'd known coming into the Lady Luck Lounge that he was going to do whatever it took to get Pricilla to notice him. He'd also known how Javier would react. Javier had been chasing his boss' sister for the past three years, and she'd been stringing him along the entire time. It was all a game to her; one she not only loved to play, but excelled at. Nathan was getting tired of the games. He wanted out. The problem was, this life was all he knew. And there was only one place he wanted to be. One woman he wanted to be with. The problem was, she wanted nothing to do with him.

Finally, pulling his gaze from Javier's, he glanced over at Bernardo. "You need to keep your dog on a leash before something happens to him."

"You fucking prick."

Nathan was ready for the fist that came out of nowhere. Blocking it easily, he landed one of his own in Javier's gut. Grabbing him by the front of his shirt, he yanked the bastard forward, getting in his face. "Out of respect for Pricilla, I'm going to let you go now. If you come at me again, you won't make it out of here alive. You feel me?"

It had nothing to do with Pricilla and everything to do with her brother, but Javier didn't have to know that. Nathan knew he needed to prove that he was strong enough to handle his own battles if he wanted to earn a place in Braxton's crew. He was hoping going up against the man's head bodyguard would get him there.

Javier stiffened, and for a second, Nathan thought he was going to make the wrong choice, but then Pricilla stepped forward and placed a hand on the other man's shoulder. "I'll help Javier with the drinks. We'll be there soon." When Nathan glanced down at her, eyebrows raised, she sent him a saucy smile. "Don't worry, handsome, my brother doesn't bite. Well, not unless you piss him off." Standing on her tiptoes, she whispered in his ear, "But I might, if you're lucky."

If he was lucky, he would be long gone before that ever happened. He didn't want the woman's teeth anywhere near his body.

Nathan watched the two of them find a place at the bar — Pricilla's head on Javier's shoulder while they waited for the bartender to notice them — before turning back to the man he really wanted to talk to. Bernardo stared at him, eyes exactly like his sister's, narrowing slightly as he raked his gaze over him. Nathan knew what he saw. The same thing Pricilla saw that made her want to drape herself all over a dangerous man she didn't know. Money, power, and a lethalness that he didn't try to hide. He wanted to impress Braxton, and satisfaction filled him because he could tell his little display with Javier had.

Bernardo held out a hand, a smile on his hard lips, his gaze cold and calculating. "Bernardo Braxton."

Nathan hesitated on purpose, giving off the impression of thinking before he acted before placing his hand in Bernardo's and squeezing firmly. "Trevor." When Bernardo stared at him, refusing to let go of his hand, he went on, "Trevor Billings," knowing that soon someone would be digging deep into Trevor Billings' past to see exactly who he was, where he was from, and how he had ended up at the lounge owned by Theodore Braxton, Bernardo's cousin. That was fine. His cover was airtight. It had to be if he wanted to stay alive. He always double checked everything himself at least two, sometimes three, times before going on a mission. His life may not be perfect right now, but he wasn't ready to enter the pearly gates, either. Not without looking into those breathtaking baby blues in Serenity Springs, Texas at least one more time.

"Trevor," Bernardo muttered, finally letting go of him. "Let's go have a seat at my table. You can tell me what brings you to my neck of the woods."

And, just like that, he was in.

 *our months later*

Harper Daley drove through the small town of Serenity Springs, fighting the anger and frustration that rolled through her. She had been in the middle of cleaning horse stalls at the ranch when she received the call. Now, instead of finishing Midnight's stall so that she could bring him in from the pasture where she wanted to move the shy, skittish mare she'd purchased the week before, she was making a trip to the Serenity Springs Police Station.

Shaking her head, she swore softly. It wasn't her first trip to the station, and she knew it wouldn't be her last. The children who lived on her ranch were there for a reason. Some came from a bad home life, others had parents who were never around to take care of them, which caused them to get into mischief they probably otherwise wouldn't, and some were foster kids with no parents or family at all. When they first arrived, they tended to act out, trying anything from stealing, to fighting, to running away. She'd never had a child she could not get through to, given enough time, but Caleb was really trying her patience lately. He'd been at the ranch for three months now, and no matter what she did, the teenager fought her every step of the way.

Pulling to a stop in front of the station, Harper put the truck in park and leaned her head back against the seat, letting it idle with the radio playing for a few minutes as she thought about the young boy. Caleb had come to her from a broken home. His parents divorced the year before, and neither seemed to have room for him in their lives, nor were they willing to try and change that. His father remarried six months after the divorce was final, and now lived with his current wife and her daughter. From what Harper knew, he spent all of his time with his new family, forgetting that he had a son, too.

Caleb's mother worked all day and frequented bars at night. She enjoyed her liquor and her men, and most of the time, did not come home at all. Caleb let it slip once that he preferred it when that happened, because when she did, you never knew what kind of shape she would be in. Not only that, but the majority of the time she was not alone. Caleb raised himself for months, until one fateful night when his mother showed up after the bars closed with one of her many boyfriends. They were both drunk and ended up getting into a fight. Caleb stepped in to try and help his mother, but he did not stand a chance against the larger man. When Caleb went to school the next day with a black eye and broken arm, the school counselor contacted child services and they made the decision to remove him from his home. They would have placed him with his father, but the piece of shit told them that he didn't want the child, which was how he ended up at New Hope Ranch.

Harper tried so hard with him, but when you went for as long as Caleb had thinking you were unloved and that no one wanted you, it was hard to accept that maybe, just maybe, someone really did care about you.

Sighing, Harper opened her eyes, lifted her head, and stared at the building in front of her. Her hands tightened on the steering wheel as she straightened in her seat. That boy in there may not realize it right now, but he needed someone in his life that gave a damn, and that someone was her. She had never given up on one of her children before, and she sure as hell wasn't about to start now.

Shutting off her truck, Harper opened the door and jumped out. Slamming it behind her, she stalked to the front door of the station and yanked it open. Walking inside, she made her way to the front desk, grinning at the pretty young woman behind it. She sat with her head bowed, her long, blonde hair covering her face as she looked at some paperwork. "Good morning, Claire. Looks like I'm back again."

The woman glanced up, a ready smile on her lips. Harper stiffened slightly, quickly realizing her mistake. She didn't know who the woman was, but she wasn't Claire. "Hello, ma'am. I'm sorry, Claire doesn't work here any longer. I'm Jessa. Can I help you?"

Harper frowned in confusion, "Where's Claire?"

Jessa shrugged. "I'm not sure, to be honest. All I know is that she is gone."

Harper shook her head, tension filling her at the declaration. "No, she wouldn't just leave. She loves working here."

She had no idea what was going on, but she remembered that the last time she was called to the station, Claire seemed more distant than normal. Harper was friends with Claire's mother, and had known Claire since she was a young girl. She couldn't just let this slide. She had to know where the girl was. Something was definitely not right. Drumming her fingers on the counter, she debated on placing some calls now, but stopped when Jessa's voice broke through her thoughts.

"Ma'am? Is there something else I can help you with?"

Harper's eyes narrowed. She knew where she was going to get her answers. "Yes, I'm Harper Daley from New Hope Ranch. Sheriff Caldwell has one of my boys here."

"Of course, Ms. Daley. The sheriff is in the conference room at the end of the hall with the kid. He said to send you back as soon as you got here."

"Thanks," Harper said shortly, turning on her heel and heading to the conference room. She would talk to either Creed or Katy Caldwell and find out what was going on with Claire, but first she needed to figure out what the hell Caleb had done this time.

Stopping in front of the closed door, Harper gripped the doorknob lightly, but could not bring herself to open it just yet. She was a strong woman, normally taking everything life had to throw at her and dishing it right back, but she was just plain tired and could really use a break right now. Shaking her head, Harper bit back another curse. All she wanted to do was go home, take a nice long bath, and maybe have a glass of wine and eat some chocolate. The stress of the past month was getting to her, and if she were honest with herself, so was not seeing *him*. God, she missed Nate Burrows so much. No, not Nate Burrows... Nathan Brentworth. The minute the image of his light blue eyes entered her mind, Harper ruthlessly shoved it back out. She could not think about him right now. She would *not*. "God, give me strength," she whispered, raking a hand through her thick shoulder-length hair. Taking a deep breath, she turned the knob and opened the door.

Creed sat at one end of the table, leaning back in the chair with his arms crossed over his massive chest. His dark gaze never left Caleb when she walked into the room. Harper knew it was a means of intimidation, one Creed used quite well, along with many others. He could be scary as hell when he wanted to. "Harper," he drawled, nodding in her direction, his eyes still on the teenager sitting across from him. "Thank you for coming down."

"Creed." Harper looked at Caleb, taking in the tightness of his jaw, the whiteness of his knuckles as he grasped the arms of the chair and the defensive look on his features. There was not only anger in his gaze, but something else. Harper's eyes narrowed when she realized it was fear. She'd never seen the child afraid before, and if she had to guess, she didn't think it had anything to do with the intimidating man sitting across from him. Lowering herself in the seat beside him, she reached over and gently covered one of his hands with hers. "Caleb, what's wrong?"

The boy's deep brown eyes widened in surprise as he looked at her before he quickly lowered his gaze to the table, shrugging his thin shoulders.

Something was definitely wrong. Glancing over at

Creed, she raised an eyebrow, "Do you want to fill me in?" Harper squeezed Caleb's hand gently, letting him know that she was there for him. He needed to know someone was in his corner.

"One of the teachers caught Caleb out in the parking lot trying to hotwire a car," Creed said, leaning forward and placing his forearms on the table.

"Did you ask him why?" Harper questioned, feeling Caleb stiffen beside her.

Creed looked from her, to Caleb, and back again. "Considering the fact that he'd just gotten into it with another boy at school, we assumed he was skipping class and running," he admitted.

"Is that what they teach you in the academy nowadays, Creed Caldwell? To just assume things without all of the facts?"

"Now, Harper," Creed drawled, frowning at her, "the boy's been quiet since we brought him in. He won't talk to anyone here, not even Katy. If he isn't going to tell us what happened, then all we can do is make assumptions."

Harper nodded, slowly tapping her fingers against the table. "So, what you are telling me is that all you really know is Caleb got into an altercation with another boy, then was found moments later supposedly trying to hotwire a car?" It didn't make sense. Caleb was only fifteen years old, just a freshman in high school. He'd gotten in trouble for minor things since he arrived at the ranch. Some fighting, refusing to do his chores, not coming home after school. But he had never committed any kind of felony. Hell, he had never even done anything similar before coming to the ranch.

"Caleb," she said softly. When he continued to stare

down at his hands, she said his name again. "Caleb, look at me." He hesitated before he finally raised his eyes to hers. "Tell me what is going on," she ordered quietly.

"You wouldn't believe me," he muttered.

"Try me."

Caleb gulped, glancing quickly at Creed before looking down at the table. "One of the other boys was picking on me," he mumbled. "He was saying I was one of the bad kids that lived at New Hope Ranch. One of the kids that nobody else wants."

Harper's heart clenched at the pain in the young boy's voice. She knew he felt like his parents didn't want him, and she couldn't really blame him. "Go on," she said quietly.

"We got in a fight. I couldn't help it," he admitted. "I was just so angry. One of the teachers broke it up. When he heard what it was about, he didn't send us to the principal's office, but he said if it happened again we would both be suspended."

"Go on," Harper urged gently. "What happened after that?"

Caleb looked up, pulling his hand from hers and nervously tugging on a piece of his shaggy, light brown hair. "I wanted to get away for awhile," he finally said. "I was going to ditch school."

Harper's brow wrinkled in confusion. It still wasn't making sense. "You were going to steal the car to ditch school?" Why would he do that? He would have had to know he could easily be caught.

"No!" Caleb told her, shaking his head, a thick piece of hair falling over his forehead. "I wasn't. I promise."

"Then, why did you try to hotwire the car?"

"Because, when I left the school, I went out the back entrance by the teacher's parking lot. I figured that would be the easiest way to get out of there without anyone seeing me because there aren't any windows back there."

"Okay," Harper encouraged, placing a hand on his arm to try to calm him down.

"That's when I saw them."

"Who?" Creed interrupted. "Who did you see, Caleb?"

"I don't know who they were. I've never seen them around before. All I know is that they had Nickolas."

"What?" Harper's eyes widened in horror. "What do you mean they had Nickolas, Caleb? What were they doing? Where were they going?"

"I don't know. I was trying to follow them, but then Mrs. Blackman came out and saw me. She took me to the principal's office and called the cops…" His voice trailed off as he looked back down at the table. "I didn't know what to do."

"Caleb," Creed said gruffly, "why didn't you tell me this when you first got here?"

Caleb looked up at him, "I figured you wouldn't believe me. No one ever does."

"I do," Harper said firmly. "I believe you, Caleb."

Creed pushed his chair back, rising quickly. "I believe you, too, son," he told him.

"You do?"

"I do, and I am going to do everything I can to find your friend. Do you think you can help me with that?"

Caleb nodded earnestly, his eyes beginning to fill with hope. "Yes."

"Do you remember anything about the vehicle they were driving?"

"It was a car. Four doors." Caleb's nose scrunched up as he thought. "Dark blue with tinted windows. They put him in the trunk." Biting his lip, he looked at Harper. "Is Nickolas going to be okay?"

"I don't know," she replied honestly, "but we are going to do everything we can to find him."

"I'm going to send some deputies to the school to canvas the area and look for any leads. Harper, if you and Caleb could stay here for a little while longer, we need to talk to him and get any information that might help us track down the men who have Nickolas."

"Of course," Harper responded quickly, her mind on Nickolas and how terrified he must be. "You find him, Creed," she ordered roughly. "You find Nickolas and bring him home. That boy has been through enough."

She shivered at the hard, unyielding look that came into the sheriff's eyes as he nodded and turned to walk out of the room.

CHAPTER 3

"*A*re you sure the intel is good?"

"It's solid."

"Who did you get it from?"

Nathan shoved down his frustration, gripping the disposable phone tightly and counting to ten before he growled, "Look, you little shit for brains. I've been doing this since before you were in diapers. I don't care who you are or who you are related to. Do not second guess me."

"Sir…"

"Shut the hell up, and write this down." Pausing for a second, he stood beside one of his living room windows and discreetly scanned the area below him before muttering, "It's going down in an abandoned building at 1021 South 15th. Midnight, next Saturday night."

"Got it."

"Get this information to Assistant Director Talbot now."

"Yes, sir."

"And Peters?"

"Yeah?"

"Don't ever question me again."

Not waiting for a reply, Nathan ended the call. He needed to leave for Braxton's house soon. He was going on a gun run with Javier, and then they had a meeting with Braxton about a drug shipment coming in Saturday. The one he'd just called his handler about.

It had taken him a full month to get a position with Bernardo's crew. His background check had been clean, or maybe he should say dirty. Dirty enough to interest Bernardo, but then he'd had to prove himself. Finally, after taking out a couple of Braxton's competition, the man had let him in, but he still kept a close eye on him three months later. Which was why the gun run was with Javier and not one of the other crew.

Javier was like a damn dog with a bone when it came to Nathan. He wouldn't back down. It was as if he was looking for any little thing to use against him, even though Nathan had made it a point to steer clear of Pricilla after that first night. He wanted nothing to do with the woman. Javier could have her. In the past, he would have played the part, strung her along just like she did Javier, but he had no interest in doing it now. His dick wasn't getting hard for that bitch.

Sighing, Nathan powered the cell off, and then crossed the room in his large, two-bedroom apartment to the bathroom in the hallway past the kitchen. Kneeling down in front of the sink, he opened the doors and carefully pried the wood off the bottom of it, hiding the phone in a small compartment he'd made the first day he moved in. No one would be able to find it unless they were looking very closely, but if they were looking that closely, it would mean they'd already discovered he was a Fed.

Carefully replacing the small piece of wood so that it covered the hiding spot, he froze when he heard the door to the front of his apartment click. Quickly shutting the doors, he reached over, and flushed the toilet, then stood and washed his hands in the sink. He knew who it was. Nosey bastard was supposed to meet him at Braxton's, but Nathan knew he couldn't pass up a chance to snoop. Good thing he'd thought ahead and rented the large, classy place instead of one of the shitholes he normally stayed in. This job required it.

"Yo, Trev, you in here?"

Nathan could hear Javier's footsteps in the hallway, and had no doubt that the asshole knew exactly where he was. "Yeah." Wiping his hands on a towel, he took a deep breath before opening the door and meeting Javier's dark gaze. He stood leaning back against the wall in the hallway, his tattooed arms crossed across his thick chest. "Didn't realize I was getting a taxi to the boss' house."

"Just wanted to make sure you were still coming."

"Bullshit," Nathan bit out, turning to enter the nearest bedroom. "You wanted to come see my place." He was surprised it had taken Braxton so long to send someone to check it out, and he had no doubt Javier was inside the apartment on Bernardo's orders. Grabbing the revolver from the top of the dresser, he slid it in the holster at his side. "Hope you like it."

"It's nice," Javier said, sauntering past him to take a long look around the large master bedroom. "Must cost a pretty penny."

Nathan shrugged, sliding a knife in the sheath hidden

in is boot, ignoring Javier's raised eyebrow. "It ain't cheap." What did he care? He wasn't paying for it. The Bureau was.

Javier clapped him on the shoulder as he walked past him again. "The way Bernardo pays, you can afford even better than this, my friend." Turning back, he grinned, "And now that you seem to have realized that it's in your best interest to stay away from what's mine, I think we are going to get along just fine."

His tone was outgoing, friendly even, but the look in his eye was anything but. He was giving Nathan a warning, even if he didn't come right out and say it. Stay away from Pricilla, or else. Nathan shrugged, grabbing his sunglasses from the dresser and heading down the hall. He already had what he wanted, his foot in the Braxton door. He didn't need Bernardo's sister anymore. Javier could have her. "Hey, man, she's yours. I get that."

Javier grasped his arm tightly, swinging him around. His eyes narrowed in warning, "See that you do."

Nathan stared down at the hand on his arm, then looked up, raising an eyebrow, his gaze not leaving Javier's until the man slowly let go of his arm. "I don't want your woman. I can get a piece of ass anywhere. But you make the mistake of touching me again, and you won't be able to."

"Fucker," Javier growled before turning and walking out of the apartment. Nathan followed him slowly, closing and locking the door behind him.

There would be no more calls to his handler from his current home. He was positive there were now listening devices in at least one, if not more of the rooms. That was good. Very good. He could play the game just as well as any of the others. Soon, it would all be over.

CHAPTER 4

*H*arper was pissed. It had been almost two weeks since Nickolas was kidnapped, and Creed was no closer to finding him than he was the first day he was taken. Not only that, but no one seemed to care, except for her. Creed said he was doing all that he could. Rayna told her they were looking into every possible lead. Jace promised her they would let her know as soon as they found anything. Cody seemed lost in his own damn world. She was done waiting. Was done crying night after night while she wondered what had happened to her boy, because that was what Nickolas had become the moment he stepped foot on her ranch. One of her children.

She needed help, and there was only one person she could think of to call. Too bad she had absolutely no idea how to get a hold of the son of a bitch, and the avenues she'd tried weren't getting her anywhere. He had connections, though, and she needed him and all of those damn connections. So, she was back at the police station, just as she had been every single day since Nickolas was taken, but with a different purpose this time.

Slamming her truck door, Harper stormed across the parking lot, yanking open the station door and stalking inside. Ignoring the frantic calls of the receptionist at the front desk, she stomped down the hall to Rayna's office. When the deputy glanced up at her, she snapped, "I want Nate's number."

"Nate?" Rayna asked, her brow furrowing in confusion.

"Nathan Brentworth," Harper growled, glaring at Rayna. "I want his cell phone number, now."

"I'm sorry," Rayna said quietly, regret showing in her eyes. "I can't give that to you."

"You can, and you will!" Harper snapped.

"I can't," Rayna insisted. "It's not because I don't want to, Harper. I would if I could."

Harper gritted her teeth, clenching her hands tightly into fists. "I need to get a hold of him, Rayna."

"I don't have his number," Rayna said softly. "They change it out every time they send him undercover."

Harper froze, fear that he was somewhere and could be in danger flowing through her. She relentlessly squashed it. "Undercover? You mean like when he came here and pretended to be someone he wasn't?"

"Yes," Rayna said, her deep brown eyes softening sympathetically. "That's what he does. It's what he's good at. He is never home for any length of time. He is always out on some sort of mission."

"Pretending to be someone he isn't," Harper spat. "Pretending to care about people that he really doesn't give a shit about."

Rayna stayed silent, not contradicting her words. Pain sliced through Harper as she thought about the way she'd felt about Nate — still felt — then it was quickly replaced by anger at the thought of how he had manipulated her, placing everyone on her ranch in danger. "That son of a bitch owes me," she growled, taking a step closer to the other woman's desk. "He owes me, and if he is so damn good at what he does, then he needs to get his ass here and pay up!"

"Harper."

"No!" Harper yelled, slamming her fist down on Rayna's desk, not even flinching when a glass that was precariously close to the edge fell and shattered on the floor. "He owes me, and I'm ready to collect on that debt!"

"What the hell is going on here?" Creed demanded, stalking into the room.

Rayna stood, holding her hand out to him. "Everything is fine, Creed."

"It sure as hell doesn't look fine," he snarled, his dark gaze on Harper.

"It's fine," Rayna insisted. Looking back at Harper, she asked, "Have you tried calling the field office in Virginia?"

"Every damn day for the last week," Harper snapped. "The response is always the same. 'Mr. Brentworth is not available right now,'" she mimicked. "'May I take a message and have him get back to you when he is in the office?'" Resting her hands on her hips, Harper took a deep breath. "But he is never in the office to return my calls. And, obviously, no one is giving him any of my messages, because I haven't heard from him. Unless he is ignoring me, but I'm pretty sure that's not the case."

"When he gets sent out like this, he goes dark," Rayna

explained quietly. "Only checking in periodically with his handler."

"And how often is that?"

"It varies, but normally, every two to three weeks, depending on what he has to relay. It's too dangerous for him to make contact more often than that."

Harper clenched her teeth tightly as she thought about what Rayna said. She knew Nate's job was dangerous, she just hadn't realized exactly what it entailed or how dangerous it really was until now. She knew he chased bad guys for a living. Hell, he was with the FBI. That's what they did. But she hadn't realized that he actually infiltrated their ranks himself. She should have. It's what he'd done to her. Taking a job at her ranch, getting close to her and the children. Her spine stiffened as she remembered the outcome of that. She'd trusted him, and he had put her children in danger.

"Well, they must not be giving him my messages when he does call in, if he has in the past week. I suggest you call them and tell them you need to get in touch with him. If it comes from you, they may just get off their asses and do something."

"Harper," Creed said, walking over to stand by Rayna. "You can't come in here and threaten my deputies."

Harper's eyes snapped to his, her body shaking with fury. "Would you rather I come in here and threaten you, Creed Caldwell?"

"Dammit, Harper!"

"Don't you dammit me," she snarled. "It's been two weeks, Creed. Two fucking weeks. You promised me you would bring my boy home. He isn't here."

"Look," Rayna said softly, reaching out to cover Harper's hand with hers. "I know you're upset. I know how you feel. I care about Nickolas, too."

"You know nothing," Harper snapped, yanking her hand away, "so don't pretend that you do. I bring those kids to my ranch, into my home, and I promise them that I will keep them safe. That nothing will happen to them. They trust me. They may have problems in their lives — things they are going through — but above all else, they trust me to take care of them. I failed Nickolas. I didn't keep him safe."

"You didn't fail him," Creed said quietly.

"I did," Harper whispered, swiping angrily at a tear that escaped. "And you are no closer to finding him than you were the day we found out he'd been taken. So, if you want to take it as a threat, that's fine. But you better get a hold of Nathan Brentwood, because if you don't, I'll be back."

Turning, Harper stomped out of the office, ignoring Creed when he yelled her name. Screw it. If they couldn't do anything about it, she would figure it out herself.

CHAPTER 5

*N*athan stood stoically beside Javier, his hands hanging loosely at his sides as he watched a large, dark-colored sedan with tinted windows pull into the warehouse, coming to a stop right after it entered. Their buyer had arrived.

He hoped like hell that Peters had done as he told him, and that they were surrounded by the FBI. He was ready for this assignment to be over with. Hell, he was ready for this part of his life to be over with. He was done playing cops and robbers. Retirement was starting to sound pretty damn good to him.

All four doors opened at the same time, and a man emerged from each one, dressed in dark suits and ties, weapons in their hands. They waited stiffly until the man in charge finally slid from the backseat. His gaze met that of his men, and then he looked at Javier, Nathan, and the rest of the Braxton crew. Stepping forward, he straightened his shoulders and demanded roughly, "Where is your boss? I came to deal with him. Not his lackeys."

Nathan stayed quiet, knowing the man was just trying to rile them up. Javier, however, did not. "Mr. Braxton is nearby," he snarled, glaring at the buyer. "Once we verify what you have is legit, he will be brought in. Until then, you talk to me."

Rafe Hernandez raised an eyebrow, a slow grin spreading across his face. "You? Really? They sent a boy to do a man's job?"

"I'll show you a fucking boy," Javier snarled, slipping a knife from his pocket.

"Stand down, Javier," Bernardo ordered, appearing from a small room a few yards away.

"He insulted me, boss. I can't let that slide."

"You can, and you will."

Javier was a hothead, but he did take orders from Bernardo. Slipping the knife back into his pocket, Javier moved closer to Nathan. "I don't trust any of these fuckers," he muttered, his hand resting on the 9MM at his side. "If they threaten the boss at all, we light this place up."

Nathan nodded, his gaze slowly going around the building. "Agreed."

Something wasn't right. His gut was screaming at him that something was off, and he learned a long time ago to listen to his gut. Suddenly, a black SUV slowly pulled up and stopped just outside the warehouse. No one got out and the engine kept running.

Bernardo took a step closer to Javier as he asked, "Friends of yours, Hernandez?"

Rafe shrugged, a sly look in his eyes when he replied, "Just a little added reinforcement."

"And why would you think you need that?"

Rafe threw his head back and laughed before gesturing

to the SUV. The doors opened and several men emerged, loaded down with guns. "Because I'm not here to make a deal with you, Braxton. I want your business. So, I'm taking it."

No sooner did the words leave Rafe's mouth, then all hell broke loose. Nathan yanked his gun from his holster as the first bullet tore into his thigh. He managed to take out two men before the second one embedded itself into his shoulder. Javier went down next to him, a bullet between his eyes. Bernardo fell beside him, blood pooling around him. Nathan grunted as pain sliced through the side of his head where another bullet grazed him. He groaned as he fought to stay on his feet.

"FBI! Stand down! Everybody stand down!"

He'd never been so happy to hear those words in his life. As the large warehouse echoed with the sound of gunfire, Nathan got off another couple of rounds before letting himself slide to the hard cement floor. Glancing around, he slowly shook his head, a moan slipping free. It was over almost before it started, with so many dead in the process. He felt the gun slip from his fingers and blinked rapidly, trying to stay conscious.

"Agent Brentworth! Agent Brentworth!"

Nathan tried to respond, but he couldn't seem to form any words. Reaching up, he swiped at his face, grimacing when pain slammed into his head and his hand came away wet with blood.

"Nathan!"

Nathan found himself lying on the cold cement floor, staring up at the ceiling, wondering if this was it. Was this how his life was going to end?

"Dammit, Nathan! Stay with me!"

Blinking, he looked up into clear, light-blue eyes. "Harper," he rasped, trying to reach out and touch her. Wait, no, Harper wouldn't be there. Not in this hell. She was back in Serenity Springs. Safe.

"Somebody get an ambulance in here, now!"

Slowly, Nathan's eyes closed and he slumped back, whispering her name one more time. "Harper."

CHAPTER 6

*H*arper sat at her desk, staring blindly at the ledger book in front of her. She had to finish paying the bills, draw up a list of chores for the children for the coming week, see what groceries they needed to buy, and so much more. She couldn't seem to make herself do any of it. All she could think about was Nickolas, and where he might be. What he must be going through.

Reaching for a file on the edge of her desk, she opened it and stared at the picture paper clipped inside. Short, thick black hair. Dark eyes full of intelligence, but also a wariness that no child his age should have. Tracing a finger down the boy's cheek, she whispered, "I am so sorry, Nickolas. It was my job to shield you from all of the evilness in the world and I failed." A tear slipped free as she went on, "I'm going to get you back, son. I don't care what I have to do; I'm bringing you home. I promise."

"Harper?"

Quickly wiping her tears away, Harper raised her eyes and smiled. "Yes, Misti?"

Misti had come to live on the ranch the year before, after an accident claimed the lives of her parents and younger sister. Normally, Harper didn't take in orphaned children because that wasn't what her ranch was about. However, when an old friend in Dallas contacted her, she'd been unable to say no. Misti had no other family, no one who cared about her, and was about to be thrown into a system where she would be lost. Harper knew what that was like and refused to let it happen to the sweet child. One meeting was all it took. Two days later, Misti moved to New Hope Ranch and had been there ever since.

"There's a cop here to see you."

Sighing, Harper closed the file and stood, wondering what one of the children had done now. A couple of them had been acting out more since Nickolas's disappearance, which meant she'd heard from the Serenity Springs Police Station on more than one occasion. Normally, it was Jace or Cody who paid her a visit, but Harper was surprised to see Rayna on the other side of the door this time. It had been a full week since she last saw the deputy, after she ordered her to get Nate's cell phone number, no matter how she had to. Seven long days full of anger and sadness as Harper tried to understand why this was happening. Why Nickolas was being put through hell again, why she was losing a child she had chosen to claim as her own.

Harper's heart began to pound as she slipped outside, closing the door behind her so they would have privacy, and then quickly made her way down the stairs where the deputy stood. "Rayna."

"Hi, Harper." The other woman's eyes were full of gentle understanding, but also a clear resolve. Whatever she was at New Hope Ranch for, it had nothing to do with the children who were currently there. This was about Nickolas.

Her hands clenched tightly into fists, Harper demanded, "What is it?"

Rayna was quiet for a long moment before she finally said, "I got that number you asked for."

Hope began to build, and Harper swallowed hard. "How?" She'd called every single day since she'd last spoke with Rayna, but no one would help her. They said Agent Brentworth still was not available, but they promised to relay her messages as soon as he was. All she could do was wait.

"I pulled some strings." Slowly, Rayna retrieved a small piece of paper from her pocket and held it out to Harper. "Harper, there's something you need to know."

Harper accepted the slip of paper, glancing at it quickly. All it had on it was Nathan's name and a number. Taking a deep breath, she raised her head to meet Rayna's gaze. "Yes?"

Before Rayna could reply, the door behind them slammed open and Misti ran out, tears streaming down her cheeks. "I hate you!" she screamed at someone behind her, losing her step and tripping down the stairs.

Harper reached out and caught her just before she went down, hugging her close. "Hey, sweetheart. What's wrong?"

"Caleb's a jerk!" Misti cried, scrubbing at her wet eyes. "He said Nickolas is never coming back. That he's probably dead by now." Looking up at Harper, her wide blue eyes covered in a sheen of tears, she whispered, "That isn't true, is it Harper? Nickolas isn't dead, is he?"

Harper held the sobbing girl close, her own heart

breaking at the thought of the very real possibility that Nickolas could be lost to them. It had been three weeks since he was taken. So much time had gone by that anything could have happened.

"Misti, I'm sorry. I didn't mean anything by it," Caleb said quietly, appearing at the top of the stairs, his voice full of guilt and regret. "I shouldn't have said that." When Misti turned her head away, burying it into Harper's stomach, refusing to look at him, Caleb scowled. "Look, I didn't mean it. I shouldn't have said it. Can't we just forget it?"

Harper saw the very real pain in his own eyes, and her heart went out to him. Giving Misti one last hug, she slipped a finger under her chin and gently lifted her head until the girl's gaze met her own. "I believe him, sweetheart. Caleb didn't mean to hurt you. He's just worried about Nickolas like we all are, and doesn't know quite how to handle it." Looking up at Caleb, Harper smiled. "We all need to stick together right now. Nickolas is out there somewhere, and he needs us to be strong for him. All of us."

Caleb nodded slowly, glancing over at Rayna before muttering, "I really am sorry, Misti."

Harper felt a small shudder go through Misti before she bit her lip and looked over at him. "It's okay. I just...I don't want to lose anyone else like I lost my parents and Hannah. I can't."

Guilt swept over Caleb's face, and he whispered, "I am such a jerk. I didn't even think about your family before I opened my big mouth."

Before Harper could say anything, Misti pulled away from her and ran up the stairs. Sliding her small arms around Caleb's waist, she hugged him. "It's okay, Caleb."

At first, Caleb looked like he might push her away, but then his own arms came around her and he held on tightly. Harper swallowed hard when she saw the wetness tracking down his cheeks, but wisely kept her mouth shut. He needed to shed a few tears for his friend. Needed to get it all out.

After a moment, Caleb leaned back. Grinning down at Misti, he tugged on one of her light blonde curls and asked, "How about some popcorn, squirt?"

Misti giggled, wiping at her wet cheeks before turning to run into the house. "Race you!"

Harper waited until Caleb shut the door behind him before turning back to Rayna. Rayna's eyes were still on the door, and there was a small frown on her face. "Rayna?"

Rayna slowly pulled her gaze from the door to look at her. "How old is Misti?"

Harper's lips tilted up into a small smile as she thought of the girl who had stolen her heart just the year before. "Eight. She will be nine next month."

"I don't understand," Rayna said in confusion, glancing over at the door again.

"What do you mean?"

"I didn't know that you took in kids that young. I thought they had to be teenagers?"

"Actually, I normally take in children twelve and older." Sighing, Harper shrugged. "Misti was a special case." When Rayna glanced back at her, an eyebrow arched in inquiry, Harper explained, "Misti's family was killed in a car accident last year. Both of her parents and her younger sister. She didn't have anyone else. A friend of mine who happened to be her social worker called me to see if I could take her in. Normally, I wouldn't have, but I couldn't stand the thought of that sweet child going into foster care."

Rayna frowned again, indecision weighing on her face. "So, you are her foster mother?"

"I suppose you could say that," Harper replied, wrapping her arms around her waist as her thoughts slipped back to the small piece of paper she gripped tightly in her fist. "Rayna, thank you for Nate's number. I really appreciate it. I'm going to go call him now."

Resting her hands on her hips, Rayna took a deep breath before saying, "Harper, tread lightly with Nathan, okay. He's been through a lot this past week."

Before she could stop herself, Harper snapped, "Really, more than what that boy is going through right now, Rayna? He was thrown in a trunk, kidnapped, and we have no idea where the hell he even is or what is happening to him now."

Rayna was quiet for a moment, then she said, "I can't give out specifics, but I will just tell you that he's been through hell. Please, don't push him too hard. Nathan is the kind of person who doesn't know when to stop. I have no doubt that the minute you call, he will be on the first flight here. That's how he is. But that doesn't mean he should be." With one last glance up at the closed door, Rayna turned and walked to her cruiser. Getting in, she left without another word.

Harper frowned, looking down at the small slip of paper in her hand with Nate's name and number. Slowly, she traced his name, fighting the tears that wanted to flow.

She had no idea what Rayna was getting at with her cryptic words. All she knew was that she needed Nate's help.

Indecision warred inside of her. She had sent him away so many months ago, but now she needed him. Nickolas was in danger, and she knew, somehow, deep down inside, that Nate was the only one who would be able to help her.

Harper slowly dialed the number, hesitating over the send button before she finally gritted her teeth in determination and pressed it. For Nickolas, she would bring the only man she had felt anything for since the death of her husband back into her life. The man who had made her feel like no other man ever had, not even her deceased husband. The man who had lied to her for months. For Nickolas, she would do it.

Nathan groaned, closing his eyes and leaning back against the pillow. They may have bagged the bad guys, even more of them than he'd set out for in the first place, but he was paying for it now. His entire body ached from his head to his shoulder to his thigh. Three bullets this time. They'd removed the ones in his shoulder and thigh and he was slowly starting to heal, but after several days spent in the hospital, he was beginning to go crazy.

The department had given him a new cell phone and he glared at it when it started to ring. He was close to throwing it across the room in frustration, but decided talking to whoever was on the other line had to be better than what he'd been doing lately. Gritting his teeth, he answered with a growl, "Brentworth."

The pain he was experiencing was nothing compared to the ache in his chest in the vicinity of his heart when he heard her voice. One he had not heard in months. One he had missed with every fiber of his being. In all of his years on the job, not once had he ever crossed that line. Never had he become personally involved while undercover... until her. She had stolen his breath the moment he saw her, and later on, his heart. Her determination to save every last kid that she could, the way she put everything she had — her heart and soul — into saving all of the children at New Hope Ranch, had captivated him from the beginning. He'd fallen, and he'd fallen hard, even though he knew it was a mistake. He had tried to fight it, but in the end, it didn't matter.

He never thought he would hear her voice again. That husky, sexy tone, that set his balls on fire.

"Nate, are you there?"

Fuck. He missed her so much. She was the only woman who had ever crawled under his skin. The only one he'd ever wanted for more than just a one-night stand. She'd torn his heart out and stomped on it. Even though he knew the reason behind her rejection, knew it was his own fault, it had still hurt. So fucking much. Everyone he worked with thought he was cold as ice, hard as steel. Someone nobody could ever reach. But... they were wrong. This woman, Harper Daley, had reached him. And even now, after all this time, there wasn't anything he wouldn't do for her.

"Nathan?"

"Yeah," he said gruffly. "I'm here."

"Nathan, I wouldn't be calling if it wasn't important."

Like he didn't already know that. She wanted nothing

to do with him after his time at New Hope Ranch in Serenity Springs, Texas. He'd put the children who stayed on her ranch in danger, something she could never forgive. He'd screwed up, big time.

"What's wrong, Harper?' he asked, his eyes going to the door of the hospital room when a nurse walked in.

"Nathan, they took him. Caleb saw them throw him into the trunk of a car, and they took him somewhere. Creed's been trying to find him, but he can't."

Nathan immediately stilled at the terror in her voice. That kind of fear could only mean one thing. The *him* she was talking about was one of her kids at her ranch. Struggling into a sitting position, he swung his legs over the side of the bed against the protests of the nurse. "Who?" he demanded roughly. "Who did they take, Harper?"

"Nickolas."

Nickolas. The boy they had saved from his psychotic mob boss father. The one person who had managed to weave himself into Harper's heart on that mission so long ago. "Who took him?"

"They don't know," Harper whispered, and he could hear the tears in her voice. "Please, Nate, I need you."

Damn him to hell. He wished she was calling for him and not the boy. "I'll be there as soon as I can."

"Mr. Brentwood, you can't leave," the nurse gasped.

Ignoring her, Nathan struggled to his feet, swaying slightly. "I'll be there soon," he repeated before ending the call. Harper needed him, and he was going to be there for her, no matter what.

CHAPTER 7

"*T*his is all my fault, isn't it?"

In the middle of placing a bridle on a hook in the tack room, Harper glanced back at Caleb. Her mind on Nate and when he might arrive, she didn't realize what he was talking about at first. "What do you mean, Caleb?"

"I should have said something to the sheriff in the beginning. I shouldn't have waited until…"

His voice trailed off, and Harper quickly hung the bridle and then crossed the room to him. Placing a hand gently on his shoulder, she said, "You didn't do anything wrong, Caleb. You were nervous. Sheriff Caldwell can be very intimidating. There was nothing wrong with waiting until someone you trusted arrived."

Swallowing hard, Caleb looked down at his dirty, worn out boots before whispering so low she almost missed it, "I do trust you."

Pulling him in for a hug, Harper murmured, "I will always be here for you, Caleb. You became one of my boys the moment you stepped foot on my ranch. Nothing is ever going to change that."

"You won't make me leave?" he asked quietly. "Even though I do bad things sometimes."

"I will never make you leave," Harper told him, and she wouldn't. No matter how much the child might aggravate her at times, she considered him family now. She would do anything for her family. "I know you've been through some things in the past, and when you are ready, I will be here to listen. But know this." Gesturing around the barn and out toward the house, she told him, "This is your home now. You are welcome here until you graduate from high school. At that time, you can choose to move on, or you can stay even longer if you would like. I always need good counselors."

"You mean it?" he asked, his eyes wide with wonder. "After everything I've done? You would keep me?"

"Caleb, you may have done some things in your life that you shouldn't have, but we all deserve a second change." Letting a slow grin cross her face as her eyes lit up, she said, "Or a third or a fourth."

Caleb returned her smile with a boyish grin, shrugging his shoulders. "I guess I'm a slow learner."

"What I am trying to say is that no matter what, you will always have a place here. We will work on making better choices, but I am not going to send you away because of the ones you make."

Caleb's brown eyes misted over with tears and he looked away. He quickly reached up to swipe at a stray one that slipped free and trailed down his cheek. "My parents did. Dad has a new family. He told me he doesn't want me. Neither does my mom."

Slinging an arm around his shoulder, Harper guided him toward the barn door. "Well, that's their loss and my gain."

Looking up at her, Caleb grinned. "You mean that, don't you?"

"You better believe it." And she did. Harper had no idea how any parent could throw away their child like Caleb's had, but she was glad she was the one there to pick up the pieces. He might be a difficult kid, but he was starting to come around. And she could tell he was definitely going to be worth the hard work.

They had almost made it across the driveway and to the house when Harper heard the sound of a truck engine in the distance. Pausing, she glanced over at the road, her eyes narrowing when a large, black pickup pulled into her driveway. Her heart began to pound and her palms became sweaty as she realized just who might have arrived only one day after she'd called him. He couldn't be there already, could he?

"Why don't you run in and help Maisy and Haven finish dinner, Caleb?"

He looked at her in concern, and for a moment, she thought he was going to refuse, but then he nodded and turned toward the house. His eyes strayed back to the truck that was slowly making its way down the drive, and he asked, "Are you sure you don't need me, Harper?"

Giving him a reassuring smile, she shook her head. "No, go on inside. I'll be there soon."

Caleb hesitated for a moment longer before turning and running up the stairs to the front door of the house. Glancing back, he called, "If you need me, holler."

Her heart filling with love for the boy, Harper nodded. "I definitely will, Caleb."

She watched until he made his way inside and shut the door firmly behind him before turning back to face the truck that had stopped just a couple of yards from where she stood. She waited impatiently as the door slowly opened and a man emerged. He was dressed in a dark blue suit and tie, the handle of a gun peeking out from a holster at his side when he moved. Tall, dark hair, greying slightly at the temples. Hard, steel-grey eyes connected with hers as he closed the distance between them. He looked so different in some ways, but exactly the same in others. That hard angle of his jawline, the thick width of his chest, the firm lips. She would have known him anywhere. Except, was it her imagination or did his skin have a tinge of grey to it? Her eyes narrowed slightly as she looked closer. And were there small beads of sweat forming on his brow? What had he been through? Why had Rayna tried to caution her? Clenching her teeth, she waited until he stopped in front of her.

"Nate."

His gaze roamed over her face as if memorizing her features, and he slowly raised his hand, caressing her cheek with his fingers. "Harper. You recognize me."

Harper closed her eyes at the feel of his skin on hers, a small shudder running through her body. God, she had missed him so much. Everything about him. But the man she missed was Nate Burrows. She didn't really know this man standing in front of her now. Did she?

Taking a step back, Harper held her head high, and her back straight as she said, "Thank you for coming Nate...Nathan."

"You can call me Nate."

"Is that who you are?"

He paused, then slowly shook his head, sighing. "No, but I want to be."

Her heart skipped a beat at his admission, and she whispered, "I think we all want to be something we aren't."

His eyes narrowing, he asked, "Do you?"

Did she? Yes, a part of her did. But he didn't need to know about that. Ignoring his question, she placed her hands on her hips and cocked her head to the side, unconsciously pushing her breasts out more. She stiffened when his gaze dropped to them and snapped, "Dammit, Nate, my face is up here."

Nathan's lips curled into a smile as he raised his eyes, meeting hers. "Sorry, sweetheart, a man can't help himself sometimes."

That low, sexy drawl was back. The one he'd used the entire time he'd lived on her ranch. The one that made her toes curl, and her nipples bead up. "Stop it."

"Stop what?"

"Talking like that!"

The grin widened and he shook his head. "I have no idea what you are talking about, Harper, but I love the way you look when you are pissed off." Leaning closer, he said, "So fucking hot."

Shaking her head, Harper raked a hand through her thick blonde hair before asking, "Have you found out anything about Nickolas, yet? He is the reason you are here."

All playfulness vanished from Nathan's face; his eyes once again hardening into steel, and he mimicked her pose

— his hands on his hips. "Not yet. I just got into town and came out here to see you first. I wanted to hear your version of what happened, and then I'm going to go talk to Creed."

Nodding, Harper turned toward the house, resisting the urge to look back at him. She had the nagging suspicion that something as wrong with him, but she didn't know what. "You'll want to talk to Caleb, then. He was the one who saw them take Nickolas."

"Caleb?"

"One of my boys. It happened while they were at school."

"Son of a bitch," Nathan snarled. "They took him from school and no one saw anything?"

Harper could feel him close behind her as she entered the house, and she quickened her steps to put a little distance between them. She didn't care who he was — Nathan Brentworth or Nate Burrows — the man still had the ability to tie her stomach into knots. Why was that? After everything that had happened, she should want to shoot him, not take up where they'd left off just a few short months ago.

"Correct. It happened in the teacher's parking lot, and there aren't any cameras there."

"Why not? What was Nickolas doing in that parking lot in the first place? And why was Caleb there?"

Nathan's voice was hard and unyielding, and Harper stopped just before they reached the kitchen, and turned to face him. He was so close, she automatically put her hand up, placing it on his chest to stop him. Mad at herself when her hand trembled slightly, she growled, "None of this is Caleb's fault, Nate. Don't be an ass to him."

Nathan covered her hand with one of his and leaned in to whisper quietly in her ear, "I've decided that I like it when you call me Nate. Gets me so fucking hard, Harper."

Her heart pounding, Harper yanked her hand from his, barely resisting the urge to smack the smile off his face.

"Harper?"

Shoving hard at Nathan's chest, she looked back at Haven. "I'll be there in just a second, sweetie."

Haven nodded slowly, her gaze going from Harper to Nathan, and then back again. "Dinner's ready. We've carried everything out back to the picnic tables. Just wanted to let you know."

"Sounds good." As soon as the teenager went back into the kitchen, Harper swung around and hissed, "You will not touch me in front of the kids; do you understand, *Nathan*?" She stressed his full name, hoping it would piss him off. "One of those girls out there is new since you've been gone. She was assaulted by a boy at her school, and I don't want to trigger any bad memories."

Nathan's face turned to granite and he gave her a nod. "Understood."

Harper didn't know if he was angry with her or the news she'd just given him, but she told herself she was glad when he backed away, motioning stiffly toward the kitchen doorway. Holding her head high, she swept through the kitchen and out the patio door to the backyard. One long table was to the left, covered in grilled cheeseburgers, chips, fries, and watermelon. There were three picnic tables, two directly in front of her and one to the right. Four girls sat at one, three boys at another, and two boys and a girl at another.

Clapping her hands, she waited until they quieted

down before saying, "This is Nathan Brentworth. He's an agent with the Federal Bureau of Investigation. I've asked him to help me find Nickolas, so he will be staying in Serenity Springs until we bring Nick home."

One of the boys frowned, his eyes narrowing on Nathan where he now stood beside her. "You look familiar."

Nathan crossed his arms over his thick chest and gave the children a small smile. "That's because I've been here before, Kyle. I helped Harper with the ranch not too long ago."

"Nate!" one of the girls squealed, a huge smile lighting up her face when she recognized him. Then she frowned. "You look really different."

Nathan chuckled, a sound she had missed over the last few months. "Yes, I do, Savannah. When I was here before, I was on an undercover mission. I had to make myself look different so that the bad guys didn't recognize me."

"Wow, that's cool," Caleb breathed, his eyes wide with wonder. "And you are going to help find Nickolas?"

"Yes, I am." Nathan moved toward the picnic table full of boys, and leaned up against it. "What's your name, son?"

At first, Harper thought Caleb wasn't going to respond, but then he straightened his shoulders and tilted his chin up. "I'm Caleb, sir. Caleb Adams."

Nathan stared at him thoughtfully for a moment, then straightened, placing a firm hand on the boy's shoulder. "Caleb, I think you are the one that I need to talk to. Is that right? You were the last one to see Nickolas?"

Caleb licked his lips nervously, and then nodded. "Yes, sir."

"Well, why don't we eat first, and then you can tell me everything you saw. That work?"

The tension seemed to drain out of Caleb and he nodded again. "Yes, that works for me."

"Good."

Taking her cue from Nathan, Harper told the kids, "Let's eat; then it's the boy's turn to clean up." While they all groaned at the thought of doing dishes, Harper moved to the table that held the food and began to fill her plate. She'd missed lunch, and hadn't realized how hungry she was until the smell of food had wafted over to her.

Taking her plate over to sit by the table full of girls, Harper rubbed a hand tiredly over her face. Lost in thought, she jumped when she felt a hand rest on her arm.

"I'm going to find him, Harper."

His voice was deep, confident, and full of promise. Something she really needed at the moment. Raising her eyes to meet his, she whispered, "I hope so."

It was dark, and the room he was being held in smelled dank and musty. Nickolas stalked slowly around the small area, anger pouring through him. He could hear the bastards in the next room, laughing and drinking, betting on who could chug the most beer. Idiots. They were just a bunch of gangbangers. Did they really think they could hold him there much longer? He was the son of a notorious mob boss. Maybe he hated that life and didn't want anything to do with it, but that didn't mean he didn't know how to live it. He'd been trained by the best, and he wouldn't hesitate to fight his way out once he found an opening. And he would find one. He was just biding his time. He might only be sixteen, but he'd done things most men hadn't.

He stiffened when he heard the sound of a key in the lock, glaring at the man who opened the door. "If you know what's good for you, you'll let me go, now."

The man threw back his head and laughed, taking a swig from the bottle in his hand. "Do you really think I'm afraid of you, you little shit?"

"Do you know who I am?"

"I know exactly who you are, little boy," the man sneered, taking another drink of the liquor. "Nickolas Cortez, son of Diego Cortez, and my meal ticket to a new life." Taking another swig, and then swiping his mouth with the back of his arm, he grinned. "And getting to fuck over that Daley bitch by taking someone she cares about is just an added plus. I can't wait until we can go back and take care of her."

Daley bitch? "What does Harper have to do with this?" Nickolas demanded, his hands clenching tightly into fists. Harper had taken him in when he had no one. The son of evil. She'd accepted him and treated him as if he was her own child. She was the mom he'd never had but always wanted. No one was going to hurt her. Not if he could help it.

"Don't you worry about her, little Nicky," the man said, laughing again. "Trust me. You are going to have enough to worry about soon."

When Nickolas took a step in his direction, the man's gaze instantly became cold and calculating. "Ah, so you want to fight? Soon…soon you will have what you want. Until then, I advise you to save your energy. Once we hand you over to the man paying us a cool million for you, you will be in for the fight of your life."

Before Nickolas could respond, he stepped back out of the room, slamming the door shut and locking it from the outside.

What the hell was going on? Nickolas walked over and sat down on the bed, leaning forward and resting his arms on his legs. It didn't make any sense. How did they know Harper? Why did they want to hurt her? Who was he being sold to? Someone who must really want him if they were going to pay these losers a million bucks.

Nickolas stood, raking a hand through his hair as he surveyed the small room he was in. He was going to have to find a way to get out, and fast. He had no idea who was bargaining for him, but right now, he had bigger things to worry about. Harper was in trouble and she needed him.

CHAPTER 8

*N*athan strode into the Serenity Springs Police Station, intent on talking to Sheriff Creed Caldwell. It was a constant battle to ignore the growing migraine along with the agonizing pain in his thigh with every step he took. He knew he needed to rest, but he couldn't take the time. Not yet. From what he had managed to put together, it had been over three weeks now, and no one had managed to locate Nickolas. It was bullshit. There was a trail. There was always a trail. They just had to find it.

"Sir. Sir, you can't go in there."

Ignoring the young woman at the front desk, he headed straight back to the office where he could hear the person he assumed was the sheriff yelling at someone. Not bothering to knock, he entered Creed's office and raised an eyebrow when the man slammed the receiver down on the phone, swearing loudly.

Creed's eyes snapped to him and he frowned, growling, "Who the hell are you, and what are you doing in my office?"

"Nathan! I wondered when you would get here."

Nathan turned to look at Rayna as she walked in behind him, a grin appearing on his face at the happy, peaceful look the deputy wore. It was something he wasn't used to seeing. Evidently, settling down in small town Texas suited her. Or, maybe it was Ryder Caldwell.

"Hey, Rayna. You're looking good."

"Thanks." When Creed grunted, obviously expecting their attention to shift to him, Rayna placed a hand on Nathan's arm and said, "This is Agent Nathan Brentworth from the FBI, Creed. He was one of the agents who helped me capture Diego Cortez and put him behind bars." When Creed continued to frown, she went on, "He was under-cover here as Nate Burrows, on New Hope Ranch."

"Ah," Creed said, leaning back in his chair and crossing his arms over his chest. "You look a lot different, Brentworth."

Nathan shrugged, placing his hands on his hips, wincing at the dull throb in his shoulder. "I was on assign-ment then."

"So, this is how you look otherwise?"

"This is the real me," Nathan said simply. "Now, as much as I would like to sit and chat with Rayna for a bit, there isn't any time. I'm here for a reason."

"Harper called you," Rayna said quietly. "You've come to help find Nickolas."

"That woman is in here every day asking about Nicko-las," Creed interjected, shaking his head. "I can understand why she's upset, but she needs to sit back and let us handle things."

"Because you're doing such a good job of it?" Nathan asked, feeling immediately defensive for Harper. "She comes in here every day because she loves that boy as if he were her own. She has no idea how to find him herself, so she has to rely on you." When Creed rose from his desk, his face darkening in anger, Nathan refused to back down. "It's been three weeks, Sheriff, and you haven't found him yet. I don't blame Harper for coming in here to make sure you are actually doing something."

"Who the hell do you think you are, coming in here and talking to me like I'm some kind of..."

"Stop," Rayna interceded, stepping between them. "Please, both of you, focus on what is really important here. It isn't either of you, or me, or even Harper's feelings. It's that sixteen-year-old boy who is out there alone somewhere, probably scared out of his mind. He is the one who matters. Not any of us."

Nathan stayed silent, watching the sheriff closely, unaware that he was swaying slightly on his feet. The muscle in Creed's jaw ticked and his eyes seemed to darken to a deep green before he finally said, "She's right. That boy's been missing for a long time, and no matter what I do, I can't seem to fucking find him. And no one wants to help."

"I do," Nathan said quietly.

Creed nodded, sitting slowly back down into his chair. "Good, cause as much as I hate to admit it, I need all the help I can get on this one." Gesturing toward the chair next to Nathan, he said, "Why don't you have a seat so we can go over everything?"

Nathan heard what the sheriff said, but he couldn't seem to concentrate. Blinking, he tried to bring the man into focus as he reached up to wipe the sweat from his brow. Man, he was fucking hot.

"Nathan?"

He heard the concern in Rayna's voice, and he tried to respond, but his head was pounding and he couldn't seem to think clearly enough to get the words to form.

"Shit!"

Rayna crying out as she tried to catch him on the way down was the last thing he heard before he lost consciousness. Maybe the doctor who chewed his ass when he signed himself out of the hospital the day before was right. Maybe he should have waited a few more days.

CHAPTER 9

*H*arper sat in the glider on the front porch, glancing at her watch for what had to be the tenth time in the last hour. Where the hell was Nate? When he left after lunch, he'd told her he was going to talk to the sheriff, then needed to pick up some things in town, but would be back afterwards. It was almost ten now.

When he had mentioned finding a place in town to spend the night, she'd reluctantly offered him the cabin he'd used before. A part of her didn't want him to stay at the ranch. She told herself it was because she needed to make sure the children were safe, and in his line of work, there was every chance he could draw dangerous people to them. But deep down, she knew the truth. She wanted to keep herself safe from the feelings she had for Nathan Brentworth. He may have been gone for over five months, and he might not be the Nate Burrows she knew and cared for back then, but it didn't seem to change the way she reacted to him when he was near. He didn't even look the same, but she was just as attracted to him as she was before, if not more. And it pissed her off.

Harper stiffened when she saw a pair of headlights coming down the driveway, followed by another. Slowly, she brought the glider to a stop and stood. The first vehicle was Nate's truck, but when it came to a stop in front of the house under the flood lights, she could tell that he wasn't the one driving. He sat on the passenger side, his head back against the seat, and didn't move when the driver's side door opened. Harper frowned when Rayna jumped out.

Creed's truck came to a stop beside Nate's, and he quickly got out, tipping his hat in her direction. "Harper."

"Creed, what's going on?"

Before he could respond, Rayna snapped, "Maybe if you would have listened to what I was trying to tell you yesterday, we wouldn't be in this situation right now."

"I don't understand?"

"I warned you that Nathan doesn't know when to stop, Harper. I told you he would push and that you needed to be careful with him right now. You obviously didn't listen!"

"What in the hell is going on?" Harper demanded, taking a step toward the vehicle.

"Like you care," Rayna spat, walking around the front of the truck to the passenger side. "All you care about is getting Nickolas back. I understand you are worried about him. We all are. But you can't trample all over others, hurting them in the process to make that happen."

"Rayna," Creed said quietly, moving over to help her. "She wasn't there. She doesn't know."

"Well, maybe she should have asked."

"Did you tell her anything?"

"It wasn't my place!"

"Would someone please tell me what is going on?" Harper interrupted loudly. "Is Nate okay?" Seeing Rayna about to snap at her again, Harper held up a hand. "Rayna, I do care, but I'm not a mind reader. You wouldn't tell me anything before, and Nate didn't volunteer any information either on the phone or when he arrived. I have no idea what is happening right now. I would never intentionally hurt someone." And she wouldn't, not even Nathan, no matter what he'd done to her in the past.

The passenger door opened slowly, and Creed rushed over to stand beside Nathan. "Easy, man. Let me help ya."

Nathan still had his head back against the seat, his eyes closed. He didn't move as he said, "I'm not gonna argue."

His voice was so quiet. Weak. She'd never heard that tone from him before. Slowly, she walked over to the truck, taking in his pale features, the way his shoulders slumped, and how he didn't make a move to get out of the vehicle. Harper's eyes widened in shock when she saw bruising around one eye going up into his hairline. Why hadn't she noticed that before? He'd worn sunglasses the entire time, but she should have seen the dark bruises on his skin at his temple. She gasped at noticing the blood stains on his light-colored slacks, her eyes flying back up to his face. His eyes were closed, his breathing shallow.

"Nate?" When he didn't respond, she tried again, moving closer. "Nate, are you okay?"

His long, dark eye lashes fluttered, and then she was staring into grey eyes full of pain before he quickly masked it. "Harper. Shit. Nickolas "

When he began to sit up, Harper placed a gentle hand on his shoulder, quickly removing it when he grunted in pain. What the hell? Where wasn't the man hurting? "Stop, Nate. You need to…"

"I need to find Nickolas."

"You can't even walk on your own right now," Creed said gruffly, moving in to stand next to Nathan, carefully nudging Harper out of the way. "You need to get some rest. Then we can hit the ground running."

"Can't do that," Nathan snarled, sitting up and swinging his legs out the door. "Fuck!"

"Nathan, the doctor said you need to be on bed rest for three to five more days."

Ignoring Rayna, Nathan slid from the truck, grasping the top of the door tightly. "So did the first ones. I didn't listen then, and I'm not listening now."

"Obviously, you should have," Rayna snapped sarcastically.

"Nate," Harper broke in, reaching up to place a hand on his cheek. "Finding Nickolas is important, but you aren't going to get far like this. Take the doctor's advice. Get some rest."

His breathing becoming slightly more ragged, and Nathan lowered his head until their foreheads touched. "Want to help you, Harper. I need to."

"You can't like this," she whispered, her hand dropping from his cheek so that she could wrap an arm around his waist.

"Where are we taking him?" Creed asked, shutting the door when Harper and Nathan began to move away from the truck.

"Cabin over there," Nathan said, pointing to one of the small cabins away from the house.

"No," Harper interrupted, steering them toward the house. "He can stay with me."

"Are you sure?" Nathan protested, leaning heavily on her. "What will the kids think?"

"I'll worry about that later." She had no idea what she was going to tell the children, but she couldn't leave him alone. She was the reason he was in the state he was right now. If she hadn't pushed for him to come to Serenity Springs, he would have stayed wherever he was before and gotten the help he needed.

"My bag's in the truck," Nathan rasped, shuffling along beside her.

"I got it." Rayna slipped past them to the truck, her gaze softening slightly on Harper as she said, "He needs to eat something. He wouldn't eat at the hospital."

Hospital? What the hell had happened? Before Harper could ask, they reached the steps and she had to concentrate on helping him up them. It took a few minutes, but finally, they were in the house, down the hall, and in the spare bedroom closest to her own.

"I need a shower."

Harper nodded, guiding him to the private bathroom in the bedroom. He stood by the door while she turned the water on. She hesitated when she went to leave, asking, "Do you need any help?"

Cocking an eyebrow, he pasted a weak but wicked grin on his face. "You sure you want to go there?"

Did she? "No." Not waiting for a reply, she rushed from the room, slamming the door shut behind her. She heard him chuckle, but blocked out the noise as she left the bedroom. Standing outside the door, she took a deep breath, raking a hand through her thick hair.

Swearing softly, she jumped when she heard a soft voice say, "I'm sorry, Harper. I shouldn't have come at you the way I did. I was just so upset after Nathan passed out in our office. And then spending hours in the hospital while we waited to make sure he was really okay, well, it took a toll on me."

Turning to face Rayna, Harper shrugged. "It's okay."

"No, it isn't." Rayna's dark eyes were filled with remorse as she went on, "Nathan is part of the reason I'm still here today. He came to Serenity Springs and helped catch the bastard who stole my life from me."

"I remember," Harper said, fighting the anger that she felt every single time she thought about the danger Nate had put the children on her ranch in just months before. "He placed every single child here at risk when he did it. There is no way I could forget."

"I know," Rayna said quietly, crossing her arms over her chest. "And I warned him when he did it that you would string him up by his balls once you found out."

"Good assumption."

"Rayna, we better get going." Creed stood at the end of the hallway, his face a mask of indifference. "Sloane is looking for me."

Rayna seemed to hesitate before reaching over to lay a gentle hand on Harper's arm. "Harper, Nathan's a good guy. One of the best I've ever met. He cares about you. If he didn't, he wouldn't have left the hospital early after being shot three times." When Harper gasped, Rayna whispered, "The man is stubborn as a mule. He's in pain, and according to the doctor here, should be in bed for the next few days. We both know that isn't going to happen. But please, try to give him some time before you go hunting for Nickolas. Losing that boy is hard on all of us, but he's tough. He's had to be growing up with a father like his. He *will* survive. Of that, I have no doubt. He will be waiting for us to rescue him from wherever he is, but if Nathan goes in the way he is now, we may lose them both."

Clenching her hands tightly into fists, Harper nodded. *Three times.* Nate had been shot three times and had still come to her when she'd called asking for his help. What other man would do that? "I understand."

Harper followed Rayna down the hall, closing the door behind the deputy and Creed, making sure it was locked before heading to the kitchen. Quickly, she warmed up a hamburger, and then added some cottage cheese to the plate. Grabbing a tall glass of milk, she placed them all on the table before making her way back down the hall. After knocking on the door lightly, she waited a moment, then slowly pushed it open.

Nate lay in the middle of the bed, naked except for a white towel wrapped around his waist, hiked up enough that it left very little to the imagination. Tears filled her eyes when she saw the dark, massive bruising on his thigh and shoulder. There were stark white bandages covering where she assumed the bullet holes were.

Crossing the room, Harper tentatively sat on the side of the bed, unable to stop herself from gently sliding her fingers through his hair, and then down the side of his face. He'd been through hell, and she'd done nothing but push him until he'd dropped. "I'm so sorry," she whispered, bowing her head as the tears slipped free. "Rayna tried to warn me, but I didn't take the time to find out what was really going on. I didn't know, but it was my own fault for not asking."

A low moan filled the air, and Nathan moved restlessly on the bed. "Harper." Her name was a breath on his lips. "Harper."

"I'm right here," she said softly, stroking her hand through his hair again. "Everything's okay."

"Have to find Nickolas."

"We will," she promised, leaning down and placing a gentle kiss on the corner of his mouth. "Sleep now, Nate. We'll find him tomorrow."

It took a while, but finally he calmed down and fell into a deep sleep. One she suspected he'd needed for a while. Knowing the house would be full of children first thing in the morning expecting breakfast, Harper found a pair of shorts and a tank top in his bag and slid them on him. It was a struggle with him being absolutely no help, but she managed to get it done without waking him up, which told her how exhausted the man really was.

Going to the closet, she took out one of the extra blankets and covered him with it. After placing one last kiss on his brow, she left the room, guilt eating at her. Guilt for not finding Nickolas yet, guilt for putting Nathan through the agony he was going through, guilt for still feeling the way she did about the man after everything he'd done. How could she trust him again? She wanted to, with everything that she was. But could she?

Nickolas stood close to the door, his dark eyes narrowed as he listened intently. He ignored the empty, aching feeling in his stomach and closed his eyes and concentrated on the voice on the other side.

"They will be here soon for the little jackass. Once we get the money for him, we can go after the bitch."

"Dude, let it go. Why do we care about some dumb broad who lives out in the boonies? Come on. Think about what we can do with all that money. Forget about her."

There was the sound of a scuffle, a loud cry, and then a dark curse. Nickolas heard a gurgling noise, and then nothing for a moment.

"What the fuck? Why'd ya do that?"

"He pissed me off. He's been pushing me ever since we picked up the kid. I don't trust him."

"So, you knifed him?"

Nickolas stiffened, his eyes widening as he realized someone was dead and he had one less abductor to get past now. Disgusted with himself that the thought of one of the bastards being dead didn't bother him more than it did, he closed his eyes tightly and leaned his head against the door.

"What do we do with the body?"

"What do you normally do with dead bodies, dumbass?"

There was silence, and then, "What about the kid?"

"What about him?"

"We can't just leave him here alone."

"He's locked in a fucking room. He isn't going anywhere. Let's get this done so we can get back here before they show up."

Nickolas waited quietly until he heard a door slam. Then he waited even longer, just to make sure he was really alone. The past few days there had been so many different voices on the other side of the wall, so many assholes that had come into the room to punch him around, that he was afraid it was a trick. How could the place be empty?

After what had to have been a full ten minutes of silence, he decided he had to take the chance that he really was alone. The opportunity might never come again. Quickly crossing the room to the old bed, he slipped his hand underneath the mattress to retrieve an old, thin piece of metal he'd found that was flat on one end. Soon, he was back at the door and working on removing the pins from the hinges. It took longer than he wanted, but finally he managed to get them free. Grasping the door tightly, he lifted it and moved it to the side.

The first thing he saw was a pool of blood not far from where he stood. His stomach churning at the site, he took a moment to look around the abandoned building to make sure he was alone, and then sprinted across the floor to the door on the other side. To his surprise, it was unlocked, and he slid outside in the dark. He was free.

Sticking to the darkness, Nickolas began to run as fast as he could, knowing he had to get as far away from where he was as quickly as possible. He had no idea how long it would take the guys holding him to come back, and whoever was paying them for him…they didn't sound like anyone he wanted to meet anytime soon. He needed to find a phone, and fast.

$\mathcal{N}$athan woke to the sound of hushed voices and the smell of bacon frying. He lay still, all of his senses slowly coming alive. His mind felt sluggish, his body sore and stiff. Where the hell was he?

"Is he dead?"

"No, you don't snore when you're dead, Misti."

Misti. Shit. Nathan froze when he realized he had to be at New Hope Ranch. But how had he gotten there? And what were these children doing in his cabin? They'd never been allowed inside when he'd worked there before. Then he heard *her* voice.

"Girls. Come out of there and let Nate sleep."

Harper. His angel. Just as suddenly, his mind shifted to the reason he was there, and it all came rushing back to him. Nickolas. The boy he'd come to find. The boy he'd failed because his pansy ass ended up in the hospital. How much time had he wasted lying in bed while Nickolas was out there somewhere, suffering?

"Is he going to live here with us now, Harper?"

The girl's voice was small, unsure. He tried to put a face to it, but he couldn't.

"No, sweetie." Harper's tone was gentle, loving. "Nate wasn't feeling well last night, and I didn't want him to be alone in his cabin in case he needed us."

Misti chimed in, "Nate's nice, Ashtynn. He won't hurt you. I promise."

Nathan's protective instincts kicked in and he had to stifle the low growl that wanted to rise in his throat. Hurt her? Those words told him more than anything else in the conversation had so far. This had to be the girl who was assaulted by the boy in her school.

Tilting his head to the side, he opened his eyes to mere slits, glancing over at the girls and Harper. Misti was alive with excitement, practically bouncing on the heels of her feet as she held on tightly to the teenager next to her. Ashtynn was petite, with wide eyes and curly, light brown hair that hung just past her shoulders. He sensed fear from her, but her next words made him realize she had a strong backbone, too.

"It's okay if he stays. If you trust him, Harper."

And that right there was the problem. Harper didn't trust him anymore. How could she after what he'd done? He didn't blame her. That didn't mean he wasn't going to do everything in his power to win her trust back, and then keep it.

Letting his eyes open all the way, Nathan smiled at the girls, hoping he didn't scare Ashtynn more by replying to her. "Good morning, ladies." Ashtynn stiffened, her nervous gaze going to his. Slowly, Nathan rose into a sitting position, pulling the blanket up with him. Harper slipped around the girls and quickly put the pillows behind him so that he could lean against them. Capturing her hand with his, Nathan held it loosely as he glanced back over at Misti and Ashtynn. Ashtynn's eyes were on his and Harper's hands, just as he'd known they would be. He was hoping if she saw that Harper accepted him, even if she might not fully just yet, and that she would begin to accept him, too. Harper must have understood what he was doing, because she took a step closer to him and laced her fingers through his.

"Nate was injured at work, girls," she told them honestly.

"At the FBI?"

Nathan nodded. "Yes, Misti. Although, I'm not sure how much longer I will be working for them. I've been thinking that early retirement sounds pretty good lately."

"Retirement?" He heard the confusion in Harper's voice. "But Rayna says you are good at what you do. Why would you retire so young?"

Nathan chuckled, shaking his head. He'd forgotten that Harper thought he was so much younger than he really was, when in all actuality, he was older than she was. "Harper…"

"Were you shot?" Ashtynn interrupted, her eyes widening, her gaze on the large white bandage on his shoulder.

Nathan nodded, suddenly sensing that he needed to tread lightly with the teenager. "Yes, Ashtynn, I was, but I'm going to be okay."

Tears filled her eyes, and she wrapped her arms tightly around her waist. "I was, too."

Nathan had to strain to hear the soft words, shock filling him at the small declaration. When Harper had told him the child was assaulted, he'd immediately assumed it had been some kind of sexual assault. Had he been wrong? When he would have said something, Harper squeezed his hand in warning, and he saw the small shake of her head.

"I was at my best friend's house one day, and a boy she knew from school came over. I didn't like him. He was mean to everyone and was always getting into fights. I told Hailey not to let him in, but she didn't listen," Ashtynn whispered, her light blue eyes filling with tears. "She liked him. Thought he was cool, but he wasn't. He was just mean."

"What happened, sweetheart?" Nathan asked quietly. When she didn't respond right away, he said, "Ashtynn, you are safe here. I promise you. No one will hurt you at New Hope Ranch."

Ashtynn's gaze flew to Harper and she nodded, scrubbing at tears that had started to slip down her cheeks. "That's what Harper said when I came here. She said she would protect me."

"And I meant it," Harper promised, her hand tightening in Nathan's.

"He brought a gun with him," Ashtynn whispered. "He said it wasn't loaded and he just wanted to show it to us, but when I got upset, he got really angry. Started yelling and screaming, saying I better shut up or he was going to make me."

Harper left Nathan's side and walked over to slip an arm around Ashtynn's shoulders, but didn't interrupt her.

"He lied. The gun was loaded. Hailey's mom walked into the room to see what was going on, and he pulled the trigger." Ashtynn was struggling to breathe as she rasped, "He killed her. The bullet went into her heart. When I tried to run, he grabbed my arm and threw me on the bed, then shot me." She was sobbing now. "He got me in the leg. It hurt so much! And then he shot Hailey. He killed her, too."

"Oh, sweet girl," Harper whispered, holding her close and running a hand gently down her hair. "I am so sorry you went through that."

"He killed my best friend," Ashtynn sobbed, clinging tightly to her. "Why would he do that? Why would he take someone's life?"

Nathan's heart broke for the sweet child who was in so much emotional pain. "That is something you may never fully understand," he said gently. "Unfortunately, we can't control the actions of others. We can only control our own."

"But he killed people," Ashtynn cried, shaking visibly. "Both Hailey and her mom are gone because of him! What if…"

"What, honey?"

Ashtynn raised her pain filled gaze to Harper and cried, "What if he comes back for me? I lived, Harper! What if he finds me and tries to kill me because he couldn't before? I don't want to die!"

"He's in jail, Ashtynn. There is no way he is going to come after you here."

"But what if he does? It could happen."

She was right, it could. Nathan had seen assholes get out on technicalities before. And if the child was a minor, there was a chance he wouldn't serve the same sentence as an adult.

"Then he will have to face me," Nathan growled.

The young girl's gaze swung to him, and he saw it begin to fill with hope. "You're staying? You'll be here if he comes."

He wasn't going anywhere if he had his way. Harper was stuck with him. She needed him, and so did these children. Nathan pulled back the blanket and slid from the bed. He heard a gasp, and looked up to see Ashtynn watching him, her face white as she stared at the stark white bandage that was wrapped around his thigh. The shorts he wore were long, but not quite long enough to cover it.

"You were shot twice?" she whispered, grasping tightly to Harper's arm. "And…you are still alive?"

"That's how tough he is," Harper said, with a small grin. "Just think what will happen if that boy shows up here."

A giggle slipped free, and Ashtynn murmured, "He wouldn't stand a chance, would he?"

"No," Nathan promised, reaching out to tug on one of her curls, "he wouldn't. So, you stop worrying about him, little one. He is nothing to you now, you hear me? He isn't worth your tears or your fear. You have me here to protect you."

"And me," Harper said.

"And me," a tiny voice piped up, and Nathan laughed when Misti's blonde head peeked out from behind Harper and Ashtynn.

"And you, sprite," he agreed.

He was shocked when Ashtynn closed the distance between them and wrapped her arms tightly around his waist. "Thank you," she whispered, before stepping back quickly.

"Glad I'm here," he said quietly, smiling gently as he watched the two girls leave the room. When he was sure they were out of earshot, he growled, "I want that little punk's name, along with Ashtynn's last name and where she's from."

"Nathan."

"Where the hell are her parents? Her family? Why is she here instead of with people who care about her?"

"Nathan."

"No, dammit!" he said harshly. "She's just a kid. She needs to be surrounded by love. She needs…"

"I know what she needs," Harper interrupted, placing a hand on his chest. "She wasn't getting it where she was. She was acting out because of her fears, and her parents didn't know how to handle her."

"Handle her? She's not a fucking animal. She's a child!"

Harper's eyes filled with tears, and she leaned into him, resting her head on his chest. "You are the first person I've met who has ever understood," she whispered. "The only one who feels the way I do."

Nathan swallowed hard, anger rushing through his veins hot and heavy at the thought of what Ashtynn had endured, followed quickly by sadness at the thought of her alone, without family. "I'm going to be keeping a close eye on that son of a bitch, Harper. I promise you, if he steps one foot out of whatever prison he's in, he will pray to God he hadn't."

Harper raised her bright blue eyes to look at him and whispered, "What happens when you're gone, Nate? We both know you can't stay. You have a life beyond Serenity Springs. A job where you do wonderful things. Where you save people."

"Maybe I just want to save the people here," he said

gruffly, tugging her closer. "Maybe everything I need is in Serenity Springs."

Before she could respond, Caleb yelled from the kitchen, "Harper, hurry up! Haven's burning the pancakes!"

Shaking his head, he leaned down and touched his lips softly to hers before turning her toward the door. "Your children need you."

She was almost out of the room before she paused and turned back. "Should you be out of bed? The doctor said you need a few days of rest."

Yes, and the doctor was probably right, but Nathan had more important things to worry about right now than sleep. He would sleep after he checked on the boy who still haunted Ashtynn and found Nickolas.

"I'm fine. Get me the information so I can make sure the kid is still doing time. I want to keep an eye on him at all times. After that, I'm going to start pulling some strings so we can find our boy and bring him home."

He saw Harper's eyes widen in surprise at his choice of words, but all she did was nod and leave quickly. That was okay. It would take a while to earn her trust back, but it would happen, and once he did, he was keeping it. He was going to prove to her that he was worth taking a chance on again.

CHAPTER 11

"*A* friend of mine out of the Dallas office is looking at all of the video coverage the Serenity Springs Police Department has from the school. I had them pull everything from three weeks before Nickolas was abducted to when he was actually taken."

"Why three weeks?" Harper asked in confusion, glancing over her shoulder at him from where she stood washing dishes.

Her mouth went dry at the sight of him. He was dressed in a snug tee shirt that hugged his large shoulders and thick chest, tapering down his abs. A pair of light-colored jeans fit his lower half like a glove, cupping the bulge in the front nicely. Her tongue snuck out to wet her bottom lip as her gaze slowly rose from where that bulge seemed to be growing, back up and over his body to where his grey eyes were darkening, filling with lust.

Breaking away from the look in his eyes, she turned back toward the sink. "That seems like a long time to go back."

"Not really. We don't know how long whoever took Nickolas was casing out the school. It could have been a month or more. We might be able to see them on one of the other cameras, in one of the student parking lots or something."

Harper paused, her brow furrowing as she thought. "But…wouldn't have Creed looked into that already?"

"I have more resources than Creed does, Harper. I called in a favor with a fellow agent. We should hear back from him in the next couple of hours."

"That fast?" Harper gasped, turning back around to face him, grasping the sink tightly and pressing back against it when she realized how close he was.

"That fast," he said, moving in even closer.

"Then what?"

"Then, as long as I get what I need, I go hunting."

Shaking her head, Harper countered, "No, then *we* go hunting."

Reaching out to slowly trace his fingers over her cheek, he muttered, "No. I need you here in case anyone calls."

"They haven't called in over three fucking weeks, Nate," Harper snapped, hating herself for leaning into those fingers. "I'm going with you."

"The kids here need you."

"There are three very capable counselors on staff who can take care of all of their needs," Harper said stubbornly. "Nickolas is the one who needs me now. I'm going with you."

The corner of his mouth turned up in a faint smile, one that put butterflies in her stomach and made her feel like a teenager. "That is just one of the things I love about you, Harper Daley."

"What?" she breathed, watching as his head lowered slowly toward her.

"Your fierceness. The way you love each and every one of the children equally here. The way you would do anything for them."

"That's three things," she whispered, trembling as he stopped, hovering just above her lips.

"And there are so many more," he said, right before his mouth claimed hers.

It had been so long since she'd felt his lips on hers, his hands roaming over her body. Even though she knew it was wrong, knew they had other things they should be worrying about right now, she couldn't fight it. She needed this, needed to *feel* again.

Nathan's hands went to her hips and he grasped them tightly, pulling her flush against his body. A deep groan rumbled from his throat as the hard length of his cock pressed into her stomach. His breathing became labored, and he grabbed the sink behind her with one hand, pushing his lower body against her. "Harper, you are so fucking beautiful," he groaned, his lips going to her neck, his tongue tracing up the side of it before he nibbled on her earlobe. "I want you. Need to be inside you."

Harper cried out, wanting more. All thought fled her mind except for the man in front of her. Sliding her hands underneath his shirt, she skimmed them up over his back, and then around to the front. His skin was smooth to the touch, with rock hard muscle right below it. She was on fire, burning up with a need she'd never felt before. "Nathan, please." Was that her breathless? Begging?

A shudder ran through Nathan's body. She felt it, reveled in it. "Where are the kids?" he rasped, pressing his hard cock into her again.

"Gone. Last day of school."

"Thank fuck."

He took her mouth again, his tongue sliding past her lips, his hand coming up to cup the back of her neck. "Anyone else around?" he demanded, after finally pulling back again.

Harper's hands went to his jeans, slipping the button free and sliding the zipper down. "No." Everyone had left the ranch for the day right after breakfast, knowing it was the last day of freedom for them for a while. Once the kids were out of school for the summer, it was all hands on deck.

Slipping the jeans down over his hips, quickly followed by his boxer briefs, Harper knelt in front of him. Glancing up, she moaned at the hungry look on his face. Grasping his hard, straining cock in her hand, she slowly moved it up and down, her heart pounding as she thought about what it would feel like inside of her.

"The front door?"

The man thought of everything, even when she could tell he didn't want to. Grinning, she leaned closer and slowly traced his cock with her tongue, from base to tip. "Locked."

"Fuck! Harper!"

Swallowing Nathan's dick down until it almost bumped the back of her throat, she moaned, loving the noises coming from his throat. He slid his fingers in her hair, cradling her head. "Harper, I need more."

Her hands slid behind to his ass, and she dug her nails

in slightly as she began to move up and down on his length with her mouth, sucking him in, and then releasing him to slid back up to the tip. He let her play for a moment, but then his fingers tightened in her hair and he took over, shoving in and out of her mouth, groaning her name. She loved it. She had a feeling Nathan Brentworth was a man who never lost control, but he was close to it now.

It didn't take long before he was warning her, "I'm close."

She moaned, digging in her nails, encouraging him to keep going. She wanted him to come, wanted to taste him.

"Harper," he gasped, his hips moving even faster. "Harper, if you don't want this, you better tell me now."

But she did want it. So. Fucking. Bad.

"Harper!" That was her only warning. Nathan stiffened, and then his dick began to pulse as he emptied it into her mouth.

Nathan stared down into Harper's clear blue eyes, small shudders running through him following his release. She was so beautiful it hurt. He loved the woman. He'd never loved anyone before the way he did her. He would live for her, die for her. Give up everything he knew, everything he was for her. Hopefully, someday she would realize that and accept him fully into her life.

Slowly, she pulled back, releasing his dick, her eyes widening when she saw that he was still hard.

"You didn't think we were finished, did you?" He wasn't nearly finished with her, yet.

Pulling up his pants, he helped Harper to her feet, and

then led her out of the kitchen and to his room. Once there, he locked the door behind them and then quickly stripped out of his clothes.

"Nathan," she whispered, slowly backing away toward the bed, her eyes dropping to his thick erection, "how can you still be...like that?"

Chuckling, Nathan closed the distance between them, catching her hand to pull her in close. "I've waited so long for you, Harper. As much as I enjoyed your mouth on me, I want to be inside you even more."

He loved how her eyes widened, her lips parting as she gasped his name. His Harper. So strong, but soft and sensual as well.

Grasping the hem of her white tank top, he took his time sliding it up her body and off. Next, went her jeans, and she was left standing in nothing but a white lace bra with a pink bow above each cup and matching panties. When she would have removed them, he stopped her. "Let me," he rasped, swallowing hard at the site of her tan, silky skin.

Reaching behind her, he unhooked her bra, sliding his hands up to her shoulders when he was done. Slipping her straps down, he followed the path of one with his mouth, nipping occasionally with his teeth. The sound of Harper's deep moan of pleasure made his dick kick once, twice. She may have taken the edge off his desire in the kitchen, but it was back full force now. Letting the flimsy material fall to the floor, he cupped her full breasts in his hands and licked his way from the soft swell of one over to her nipple. He swirled his tongue around it before sucking it into his mouth, while he tweaked the other nipple between his thumb and forefinger.

"Nate, please," she cried, scraping her fingernails down his back. He fucking loved that. It was a huge turn on to have her nails digging into him.

"Please what?" he teased, pulling away from one nipple to give the other one his full attention. Licking, sucking, nibbling.

"Nate!"

"I love it when you call me Nate," he confessed, trailing kisses down the soft, silky skin of her belly as he knelt before her. "No one else ever has. The way you say it is so sexy."

"Nate!" It was louder this time, her hands in his hair as he licked her navel, sucking gently on the skin.

He grinned, slipping his hands in her underwear and sliding them down her long, slender legs. When she tugged on his hair, trying to move him closer to her, he laughed. "Ask nicely," he purred, licking the skin right above her mound, smiling in appreciation at the trimmed blonde hair. She was perfect.

"Nate, please. I need you."

Unable to resist any longer, Nathan grasped her hips and held her still. Leaning in, he spread her lips and licked up the middle of the slit, groaning at her taste. So fucking good. When she tried to move, he tightened his grip, pausing until she gave in. He licked and sucked, loving all the noises coming from above until she flew apart just moments later, screaming his name.

He rose, his mouth finding hers as he walked her backwards to the bed. "I need to be inside you," he groaned, helping her on the mattress.

"Yes," Harper gasped, tugging him down on top of her.

Finding her lips again, Nathan raised up on his knees

and lifted one of her legs. He mapped her mouth with his tongue, then slipped it inside at the same time he slid into her slick heat. A shudder raced through his body as pleasure swamped him.

Gasping, Harper tore her mouth from his, tilting her head back as she cried out. She was so tight, it felt as if she were strangling his dick, and he couldn't get enough of it. He lay still, afraid he might have hurt her, but soon she was moving her hips, moaning his name.

"You okay?" he grunted, fighting the urge to slam into her. She was so hot, so wet.

"Move!" she ordered, digging her nails into his ass while lifting her hips as if to force him to move.

"Harper!"

He couldn't stop himself. He pulled back, then pushed deep inside, coming up with a slow rhythm. "Harper," he rasped, "you feel so fucking good."

"Yes!"

Soft moans were coming from her, and it spurred him on. He loved the sounds she made, loved the way her breasts bounced as he shoved in and out of her, the way she clung to him, urging him to move faster. A thin sheen of sweat covered his body as he clutched tightly to the sheet with one hand, holding her leg up with the other. He was so deep in her, so on fire with the lust raging through him.

When she finally screamed his name and he felt her begin to pulse around his cock, he was so far gone that he was right behind her. With a deep groan, he came, emptying himself inside of her. Breathing heavily, he lowered his head until he was resting on her shoulder, his entire body shaking. He couldn't remember ever feeling this good in his life.

Harper ran her fingers up and down his back, and he was on such a high that it took awhile for him to realize something was dripping down his leg. "Shit."

"What is it?" she asked softly, holding him close.

"I may have overdone it," he admitted, sliding off to the side of her to lay on his back, an arm across his eyes. He winced as he came back to reality and felt the aching in his body once again.

"You're in pain?" Harper asked, tracing a finger gently around the wound on his thigh.

He grinned, removing his arm so he could see her face. Cupping her cheek, he muttered, "It was so worth it."

CHAPTER 12

*N*ickolas slipped into the small café, his gaze skittering around the place as he tried to keep an eye out for the gang who had taken him. He'd been on the run since the night before, moving around Dallas, hiding in plain sight. A trick he had learned from his father. He needed to call Harper, but he was afraid to draw attention to himself. He couldn't wait any longer. He had to warn her.

"Are you okay, young man?"

Nickolas froze, turning toward the low, hushed voice. He swallowed hard when he saw the badge on the guy's hip, old habits making him want to shy away from anyone in law enforcement. His head slowly rose to meet the hard, unyielding eyes of the man in front of him.

Nickolas flinched when the cop reached out and placed a gentle hand on his shoulder. "Do you need to go the hospital?"

Nickolas flinched, pulling away from him and shaking his head. He knew what he must look like. The thugs in the gang had taken turns beating the shit out of him over the past few days. They said they were being paid for him, but as long as he was alive, they would get their money. He wished he would have thought to clean himself up in one of the bathrooms he'd stopped in. There wasn't much he could do about the bruising, but he was sure he was sporting dried blood. He'd felt the skin on his temple split open after the last jerk visited him, and he knew his lip was bloody and swollen. But, the only thing on his mind had been hiding from his captors and finding a place to call Harper from. Which was why he'd stopped in the café in the first place. He didn't have any money, but he was hoping they'd let him use their phone.

"How about some food?"

On cue, his stomach growled, loud and embarrassing. Ignoring it, he shook his head. "I'm fine." He couldn't trust anyone. That had been drilled into him at a young age. There were only two people in his life that he even remotely trusted, and only one of them fully. Harper. She'd saved him. Taken him in when he had nowhere to go. Treated him like he was someone special, even though he wasn't and didn't deserve it.

"You're not fine," the cop said quietly, dipping his head so only Nickolas could hear him. "Look, kid, I want to help you. I don't know what is going on, but you are obviously in some kind of trouble."

Nickolas eyed him closely, trying to judge if he was being sincere. His dad had several cops in his back pocket. He knew anyone could be bought. But, this guy seemed genuine.

His gaze going around the café again, Nickolas noticed it had cleared out some. There were only a couple of customers in the back, talking with their heads close together, and one other guy sitting in a booth, his eyes on them.

"Don't worry about him. He's with me."

Nickolas nodded slowly, "I need to make a phone call."

When the cop took out a cell phone and handed it to him, no questions asked, Nickolas tentatively took it. Unsure what to do, he stared at it for a moment. Was it safe to call Harper on the cop's phone?

"Look, kid, you obviously need some help. I could haul you down to the station and let them figure out what to do with you, but I'm choosing to trust you to make the right choices. Let me help you."

Nickolas gripped the phone tightly, shaking in fear and uncertainty. He should run. Just hand the phone back and get out of there. They wouldn't be able to find him. They probably wouldn't even try. But, he needed the phone to warn Harper. She was more important than he was. To him, she was everything.

Raising his gaze to meet the cop's, he nodded. "Thank you, sir."

A smiled crossed the man's face, and his eyes softened, making him seem more approachable. Holding out a hand, he smiled, "Detective Flannigan."

Squaring his shoulders, Nickolas placed his hand in the detective's. "Nickolas."

"How about we get you some food while you make that call, Nickolas?" When Nickolas agreed quietly, the detective motioned to the waitress at the counter. "Flora, how about a hungry man's skillet for my friend here?"

Smiling kindly, the woman said, "Coming right up, Detective."

Nickolas slowly followed the cop back to his booth, nodding to the other man who sat there. When Detective Flannigan motioned for him to get in, he shook his head. Understanding lit the man's eyes, and he slid in himself. "Grab a chair, Nickolas. These booths aren't big enough for two men, let alone three."

Unsure why the man was being so nice to him, Nickolas hesitantly grabbed a chair and moved it to the side of the booth. His gaze roamed the café one more time, and then the streets beyond the window, before he finally sat down.

"Make your phone call, son."

Tears filled his eyes, but Nickolas fought them back. It had been a long time since anyone had called him son, and never using that tone. Kind, caring. No, his father had been hard and cruel, trying to mold him into someone he would never be. The first time he'd known kindness was with Rayna Williams, a woman his father had ordered him to kill. She was the first one to save his life. Then Harper had stepped in, and all she'd been was kind to him.

Glancing down at the phone he still clutched tightly in his hand, he blinked back the tears. Harper had saved him from everything else, including himself at times. Now, it was his turn to save her.

CHAPTER 13

"*I* just heard back from my contact."

Harper stiffened, not realizing Nathan was in the barn with her until he spoke. She'd been hiding from him, and from her feelings. The man tied her in knots. As much as she tried to tell herself what they'd shared was just sex, she knew differently. Her heart was involved, and she believed his was, too.

Running a gentle hand down the skittish mare's side, Harper murmured softly to her before glancing back at Nathan. "Yes?"

"I think we've figured out who has Nickolas," he said quietly. "Do you know a man by the name of Julio Jarez?"

Harper's eyes widened, her heart beginning to pound as she nodded slowly. "Yes. He's part of a gang from the Dallas area."

"You've tangled with him in the past."

It wasn't a question. It was obvious Nathan already knew the answer.

"Yes."

"Tell me what happened."

"You already know, don't you?" Although, there was no way he knew everything. No one did.

"Yes, but I want to hear it from you."

The mare neighed softly, and Harper murmured, "It's okay, sweet girl," patting her neck gently. Giving her a hug, Harper closed her eyes and held on tightly for a moment. As much as she hated to revisit that time in her life, she didn't have a choice. Nickolas needed her.

"It was just after my husband's death," she whispered, resting her head against the horse's neck. "I was going through a tough time. Losing him was very hard on me. He was my best friend, the one I shared everything with, and he was gone. I had no one."

"What happened?"

"I was a psychologist with my own practice, specializing in teens with suicidal tendencies. A young teenage girl showed up at my office late one evening. I was working late, avoiding the large empty house I lived in. She didn't have any insurance, no way to pay for my services, but I decided to talk to her anyway. I could tell she needed help. That something was really wrong."

Harper paused, remembering back to the day Rosa Jarez walked through the front door of her office. Long brown hair, big brown eyes full of fear and trepidation, hands that trembled uncontrollably. There was no way she could turn the teenager away.

"Harper, what happened next?" Nathan encouraged quietly.

"Nothing, at first. We sat in silence that day for a full hour. She cried the entire time. When she left, I was sure she wasn't going to come back, but she did. Every single day, at exactly the same time, for a full week," Harper said. "And, just like the first time, we sat in silence. No matter what I said, she wouldn't talk."

"She was scared of something, or someone."

"Yes," Harper agreed, rubbing her cheek against Whisper's neck. "Her brother."

"Julio."

Raising her head, Harper met his gaze. "He was nothing more than a street thug back then, Nate, but she was so terrified of him. He had become part of a gang two months before and would do anything they wanted. And they wanted Rosa."

"Shit."

"That sweet fifteen-year-old girl. She was so scared out of her damn mind that he was going to hand her over."

"And, did he?"

"He tried to," Harper said, her voice changing to steel. "Unfortunately, for him, she began talking after that first week."

"What did you do, Harper?"

Harper shrugged, trailing a hand over Whisper's back to calm her, knowing the mare was sensing her turbulent emotions. "Like I said, I was in a bad place back then myself. I shouldn't have been seeing any clients. I should have immediately sent Rosa somewhere else. But, I didn't. I knew no one would take her on because she had no money, no insurance. I made it my personal mission to help her."

"What did you do?" he repeated quietly.

Lifting her head high, Harper said, "I hid Rosa from him, and made sure he would never find her. Ever."

Frowning in confusion, Nathan asked, "What do you

mean you hid her? From the information my contact found, Rosa is dead."

"She is," Harper agreed, "to the world she used to know."

"Tell me."

Her jaw clenching, Harper stared off into space, lost in thought, before finally responding. "I got a frantic call at home from her one night."

"She had your home number?" Nathan interrupted. "I didn't know psychologists gave their private numbers out to their patients?"

"I'd never done anything like that before. Like I said, I got more involved than I should have." Her thoughts on that night, Harper went on, "She was sobbing, scared to death. She said her brother had found out that she was coming to see me. She'd thought she was being careful, using different routes to my office each day. When she saved my numbers to her phone, she used a friend's name. She didn't tell anyone else about it, not even her mother."

"He was having her followed." It was a statement, not a question. It was the only reasonable explanation.

"Yes," Harper said quietly. "It didn't matter what way she came to my office, one of his buddies was always watching her. I guess they were just waiting until she was sixteen before putting their plan into action for some reason. Something to do with a rite of passage. They were going to make taking her virginity some kind of sick ritual or something." Meeting his gaze, she whispered, "That day was her sixteenth birthday. January sixth. I will never forget it."

"Keep going," Nathan encouraged, when she paused, sucked back in time. "You need to get it all out, Harper."

Suddenly, she realized what he was doing. He already knew most of what she was going to say. The only thing he hadn't known was that Rosa was still alive. Now, he was trying to help her through it. Help her face the past.

Taking a deep breath, she said, "She was so terrified on the phone. Told me to run, that they were coming for me. Then, I heard a commotion, something on her end. A door smashing, angry voices, and the line went dead. At the same time, my own door downstairs was smashed in, and someone yelled that they were coming for me." She had been so scared, not for herself, but for that young girl and what was happening to her. "What they didn't know, was that I had a gun and grew up knowing how to use it. None of them survived."

"There were five of them," Nathan muttered, staring at her in awe.

"They were idiots," Harper spat, shaking her head, then running a calming hand over Whisper once again when she shied away from her. "They came at me thinking they had the upper hand. As if I was some helpless female who couldn't take care of herself."

"Or a child, like Rosa."

Harper nodded stiffly. "They quickly learned they were wrong."

"The neighbors called the cops?"

"Yes," Harper said, one of her hands clenching into a tight fist. "Which meant I couldn't get away to help Rosa. They kept me for hours. I wanted to tell them about Rosa and what was happening, but she begged me not to go to the cops one night in one of our talks. She was worried for her mother. When I tried to explain to her I thought it was best if she told someone just in case something happened, she said that was why she was telling me. So, against my better judgment, I kept my mouth shut and let the police believe it was a home invasion and I was defending myself from robbers. I went to Rosa's house as soon as they let me go, but she was gone. I had no idea how to find her."

"Her mom?"

"I later learned that her mother was out of town visiting relatives, and Julio was supposed to be taking care of Rosa. She was coming back the next day so they could celebrate Rosa's birthday together."

"That didn't happen."

"No. I watched the house for a full forty-eight hours. The mother came home, but neither Julio nor Rosa did. Three days later, I received a text from Rosa, asking me to meet her in an abandoned warehouse downtown."

"How did you know it was her?"

"I didn't for sure. There was an R at the end of the text, the same way she always ended her texts to me before, but I had no idea if it was really her, or if it was Julio impersonating her. I hadn't heard anything from him or his gang after I took out the ones that came to my house."

"But you went to that abandoned warehouse anyway, didn't you?" Nathan guessed, his eyes darkening to a stormy grey. "You put yourself in danger to try and save that child, not knowing if it was really her. Dammit, Harper, you didn't even know whose phone she was using to call you."

"Yes." She wouldn't deny it, and she would do it all over again. Rosa was worth it. "I waited until it was dark, and then headed to the place in the text. I was armed and was reasonably certain I could shoot my way out of anything that might happen. Like I said, I was raised with a gun in my hand. My daddy made sure I could take care of myself. So, I went. I parked a mile away, going the rest of the way on foot. It was dark, cold, and scary as hell. It took me two hours, but I finally found her hiding behind several pallets, battered and broken, hardly able to move."

"Did they…?"

"No," Harper said, "thank God. They were so angry with her by then, they spent their time beating her, threatening her mother, telling her they were going to kill her. She had a broken arm, several cracked ribs, her jaw was broken. She couldn't talk."

"But you didn't take her to the hospital?"

"No." Harper gave the mare one last pat, and then moved toward him. "I couldn't, Nathan. They would have called her mother, who would have contacted Julio, and I couldn't let that happen. I made a call to a doctor friend of mine and took her there. We stayed with him for several days while he did everything he could to try to help Rosa."

"And then?"

"And then I hid her somewhere no one will ever find her again. Not until it is safe."

"Harper, when will that be?"

Harper shrugged. "I guess when Julio is gone. Until then, we bide our time. Rosa's happy. As happy as she can be. She misses her mother, but she knows the importance of why she can never contact her."

"And you, Harper?"

"Me, what?"

"Are you happy?" Nathan asked, seeing more than she wanted him to see.

"I have everything I could want right now, Nate."

"You left your practice."

"Because I had a new purpose. After helping Rosa, I decided it was time to follow my own dreams. I closed my practice, sold my house, and moved to Serenity Springs. New Hope Ranch is my life now. It means everything to me. I live for these children and will do everything in my power to help them become who they are meant to be."

"And to save them from not only themselves, but anyone else who threatens them."

"Yes." Closing the door to Whisper's stall, Harper walked over to a bale of hay and sat down, unable to stay standing as one thought filled her mind. "This is my fault, isn't it? Nickolas was taken as payback for what happened years ago with Rosa?"

"I think so," Nathan confirmed, sitting down next to her. "At least, that's part of it."

This was all because of her. Nickolas was in hell, going through God knew what because of her.

"Harper, stop," Nathan said gruffly, taking her trembling hands in his. "Yes, I think part of it has to do with what happened between you and Julio, but not all of it. There's something bigger at play here. You are just a pawn in all of it."

"I don't understand."

"From what my contact says, they've been monitoring anything and everything that has to do with the Cortez family since Nickolas' father was put in prison. They picked up on some chatter out there in cyberspace that indicates someone wants Nickolas, and it isn't Julio."

"What?" Her heart began to pound at what Nathan was implicating. "Someone larger than Julio is after Nickolas?"

"Yes. We think Julio nabbed him for the money and getting back at you was just a bonus."

Harper covered her mouth with her hand, terror filling her. "Nathan, we have to get Nickolas back. If Julio has him, who knows what he's done to him so far. But if what you think is true, whoever else is after him could be out for blood. It could have something to do with his father, and the people who hate his father are ten times more dangerous that Julio Jarez. We have to find him."

"I agree."

"What do we do?"

Before Nathan could reply, Harper's cell phone began to ring. Fishing it out of her pocket, she glanced at the number, frowning when she didn't recognize the area code. Her gaze flew to Nathan's as she hit answer and put the phone to her ear. "Hello."

"Harper?"

"Oh, my God! Nickolas! Is that you?"

"Harper, you have to call the cops right now. They're coming for you. You need to go to town and have the sheriff protect you."

"Nickolas, slow down. Where are you? Are you okay?"

"Harper, please, you have to get somewhere safe!" Nickolas's voice sounded so unlike him. Gruff and full of fear. "Please, Harper. I can't lose you. You're all I have left."

"You aren't going to lose me, sweetheart," Harper promised, clutching the phone tightly. Her gaze swung to Nathan, and she said, "I'm not alone. I have someone from the FBI with me. The big guns. He won't let Julio and his gang hurt me."

"You know about Julio?"

"Yes. I'm so sorry, Nickolas. They took you because of me."

"No, they didn't. They took me because some other jerk wants me, but I got away."

"Where are you? Who's with you?" Harper demanded, rising from the haybale and stalking toward the door, Nathan on her heels. "Tell me, Nickolas. Nate and I are coming to get you right now."

"Nate?"

"I told you, we have the big guns on our side."

"He's the one with the FBI?"

"Yes."

Harper heard a deep voice in the background say, "Let me talk to her, son."

There was silence, and then, "Ma'am, this is Detective Chance Flannigan. I'm in Dallas visiting family and ran into young Nickolas at a diner where we were eating lunch. He looked like he could use a little help, and here we are."

Tears filled Harper's eyes and she paused, halfway between the barn and the house. "You're a detective?"

"Yes, ma'am."

She knew she was out of her element, and that she wasn't the one he needed to be talking to now. "Nickolas is in a lot of trouble, Detective. He was kidnapped weeks ago by a gang that I've had dealings with in the past. But someone even bigger than them wants him. Can I trust you to look after him until I can get to him?"

She sat in terrified silence until she heard, "I will guard him with my life."

Taking a deep breath, she said, "I'm giving the phone to Nathan Brentworth with the FBI, so you can coordinate everything with him. Please, Detective, tell Nickolas we are coming for him."

Nathan motioned toward his truck as he took the phone from her and ran to it. "Agent Brentworth here," he growled, yanking open his door and climbing in. "I don't know who you are Detective, but you hold the life of a boy who is very loved here in your hands. Nothing better happen to him before I get there."

CHAPTER 14

*N*athan entered the hotel room in front of Harper, scanning the place before allowing her in. "All clear."

"Nickolas," she gasped, rushing past him to get to the boy who stood by the window, his eyes filling with joy at the sight of her. She wrapped her arms around him, holding him tight, as she whispered his name again. "I was so worried."

"Me, too," he said gruffly, putting his arms around her awkwardly. "When he said they were coming after you once they sold me off, I knew I had to get away and warn you."

Leaning back, Harper smiled tremulously at him, sliding a lock of dark hair off his forehead. "You don't worry about me, Nickolas. I can take care of myself."

"She can, too," Nathan said, moving forward. "You ever seen this woman with a gun?"

Nickolas eyed him warily, removing his arms from Harper and moving to stand in front of her. Nathan felt a sense of pride enter him at the sight, even though he'd only met the boy once a few months ago. It was in the hospital room where Nickolas lay in a bed after being shot while protecting Rayna. The kid was nothing like his old man. He had a goodness in him his father would never have.

Sticking out his hand, Nathan said, "I'm Agent Nathan Brentworth with the FBI, Nickolas. We met a few months ago in Serenity Springs after your father was taken into custody."

Nickolas eyed him critically before stating, "You look a lot different than you did then. Better."

Nathan grinned, waiting patiently for the boy to take his hand. "I was undercover then on Harper's ranch. In disguise. This is the real me."

"You didn't want Harper to take me in."

"It's not that I didn't want her to, Nickolas. I just wanted to make sure it was safe first. Your dad is a very dangerous man."

"Even from prison," Nickolas muttered.

"Yes," Nathan agreed, "I suspect he is just as dangerous in prison as he is out in the real world."

There was a beat silence as the boy watched him carefully, and then he slowly slid his hand in Nathan's. "Nickolas Cortez."

Nathan saw him wince when he said the last name, and he squeezed his fingers gently. "Don't be ashamed of the name you were given, son. You have no control over your father and the things he's done. You are not him."

"I don't want to be."

"Good."

Nathan let go of his hand and turned toward Detective Flannigan. "Detective, thank you for watching over Nickolas until we could get here. I know you don't have juris-diction in Dallas, but you agreed to help us anyway. I won't forget it. If you ever need anything, contact me."

"This isn't over, yet," the detective said, his gaze going to Harper and Nickolas, before coming back to Nathan. "What can we do to ensure their safety?"

"We?'

"I never leave a job unfinished."

A slow grin spread across Nathan's face, and he walked over and slapped the man on the shoulder. He wouldn't tell the man, but he'd called his contact and had the detective thoroughly vetted in the time it took him and Harper to reach Dallas. Chance Flannigan was a good man, and an even better detective. "I'll take all the help I can get on this one, Detective. Have you ever been to Serenity Springs, Texas?"

The detective's answering grin lit up his dark green eyes. "No, but I'd love to. I'm friends with the town coro-ner. Would love to stop in and say hi."

"You know Lacey?" Harper asked, slipping around to stand beside Nickolas.

"Yep."

"You know she's seeing someone?" Harper asked shrewdly.

The detective threw his head back and laughed before walking over to the bed to grab a bag off it. "Yes, I know, and I'm very happy for her. Now, let's go hurry up and wait for some bad guys."

"I don't think we will have to wait long," Nathan said, opening the hotel door and glancing cautiously down the long hallway. "I'm sure they will be heading to New Hope Ranch once they give up on finding Nickolas here."

"Yes," Nickolas agreed quietly, moving closer to Harper. "Some of them just wanted the money from whoever was paying them for me, but not Julio. Julio wants Harper." He glanced over at Harper, his eyes full of remorse. "Dead."

CHAPTER 15

*H*arper sat in a two-person glider on the front porch, a cold glass of iced tea in her hands. They'd been home for a week now and hadn't heard anything out of Julio and the rest of his gang. She knew better than to let her guard down. They would be coming, and she would be ready when they did.

"How are you doing?"

Nathan's deep voice rolled over her, soothing the tension running through her body. He hadn't left her side since they'd arrived in Serenity Springs. They'd moved the children and counselors over to Rayna's farm. Even Nickolas, although he argued vehemently about it. He wanted to stay with them to help protect Harper, but Harper couldn't allow it. She would never forgive herself if something happened to him, especially after what he had already been through. He was still recovering from the beatings the bastards had given him.

"I'm okay," Harper said, her gaze wandering over the

ranch. "I just wish they would show up and get it over with. I miss the kids."

Nathan sat down beside her on the glider, sliding an arm over her shoulders and tugging her close. "I know you do, sweetheart. We'll get them back soon."

"We?" she whispered, resting her head against his chest. He said things like that sometimes. Things that made her think he might never leave. Made her hope he planned on staying, even though she knew it wasn't fair to ask him to give up everything in his life for her. From what she'd been told, he loved his job. How could she ask him to leave it behind, even if she wanted him to more than anything else?

"We," he replied, kissing her gently on the top of the head. Taking the glass from her, he set in on the small table beside him, and then kicked his feet to make the glider move. "Harper, I called and talked to Assistant Director Talbot this morning. I told him once this is over, I will be making one last trip to the office to give him my letter of resignation and turn in my gun and badge."

"What?" Harper gasped, leaning back to look up at him. "But you love your job, Nate. Why would you do that?"

"Because I love you more," he said softly. "You have become all that is good in my life, Harper Daley. I want to spend every single day I have left on this earth with you."

"Oh, Nate."

Nathan growled playfully, leaning down to nip at her bottom lip. "You know it drives me fucking crazy when you call me Nate."

Harper grinned, sliding her arm around his waist and leaning in closer. "Yeah, that's why I do it."

Nathan groaned, covering her mouth with his.

"Well, well. What do we have here?"

Harper stiffened, her eyes narrowing when she recognized Julio's voice, a calmness falling over her. It was about damn time the scumbag showed up. After one last look into the grey eyes she'd grown to love, she sat back in her side of the glider and raised her eyebrows, her gaze on the man in front of her. She'd never actually met the guy before, but she'd heard his voice. She would never forget it. "Julio Jarez. I haven't heard from you, or even thought of you in ages. What brings you to my ranch?"

Raising a gun to point it at her, a wicked grin crossed Julio's face. "A couple of things. First, my boys are gonna have a little fun with you. Then, I'm gonna kill you; nice and slow. I'm going to make you pay for coming between me and my little sister. After that, I'm gonna find Nicky boy and take him to the men who are paying a pretty penny for him."

"There's only one problem with that, Jarez," Nathan said, stopping the glider with both feet and slowly rising to his feet.

Julio laughed, turning the gun on Nathan. "What? You, old man? You think you can stop me? You want to be a hero? I have a fucking gun, or didn't you notice?"

"Oh, I noticed," Nathan drawled, resting his hands lightly on his hips.

"Julio, hurry up and get this done, man. I want to play before we find the boy and get out of here."

Harper's gaze went to the three men coming up behind Julio. Two held knives, their eyes quickly dismissing Nathan to look hungrily at her. The other one looked so young, nervous, and uncertain.

"I want a piece of her first," one of them said, licking his lips, his dark eyes looking her over.

"Julio, I think we need to…" the nervous one started, stopping abruptly when one of the others smacked him in the side of the head.

"I don't give a fuck what you think, Trey," Julio snarled, rage flowing from him. "I'm in charge here. I'm going to kill the bitch's man first, then we are all taking turns with her before she dies. You got a problem with it, I will add you to my death list."

When Trey's gaze skittered to Julio and his friends, then back to her, she knew he was about to do something stupid. "No," he spat, "I didn't sign up for this shit. I'm not going to be a part of killing anyone."

Julio's eyebrows raised, and his gaze shifted from her to look at his buddy. "You didn't sign up for this shit? Exactly, what did you think being a part of a gang meant? Playing board games all night? Drinking hot chocolate?"

Trey's brow furrowed, and he shook his head slowly. "No, I thought it meant I was finally getting a family," he admitted.

"We are a family, kid," one of the others said, clapping him on the shoulder.

"Not any family I want to be a part of," Trey said quietly, moving away from him and glancing over at Harper. "I don't want to hurt anyone. Or kill anyone."

Harper's heart went out to the boy who just wanted a family. He'd unfortunately turned to the wrong people for one, and now could die for it.

"Either you are with us, or not," Julio said, his gun moving from Nathan to the young man.

That was his mistake. The minute the gun was off him

and Harper, Nathan made his move. A shot rang out as Nathan slammed into Julio, taking him down the stairs and to the ground.

Harper heard one of the men grunt as a dark red stain appeared on his chest. Chance Flannigan had joined the party, moving quickly toward them from where he'd been watching from one of the small cabins not too far away.

When he turned his gun on Trey, Harper yelled, "No!" Springing from the glider, she quickly crossed the porch and tackled the boy to the ground just as a bullet whizzed by her head.

"Dammit, Harper!" Chance hollered, ignoring Nathan's fight with Julio, clearing the steps two at a time to get to her.

"He's innocent," she snapped, covering the boy's body with her own. "Don't hurt him!"

She heard another shot ring out and glanced wildly around to see the other man who'd come with Julio fall to the ground next to her.

The body beneath hers shook, and the boy began to cry. He couldn't have been more than seventeen. He should never have been with Julio. Never been in the middle of gunfire like this. "It's okay, Trey," she soothed gently, refusing to move from him, keeping him safe. "You are safe. I'll protect you."

Harper heard a loud grunt, and looked up to see Chance's eyes widen with surprise, his gaze going to where a bullet had slammed into his shoulder. "Son of a bitch! We missed one!" Before she could rise to her feet, he ordered, "Stay down!"

"Harper, you better fucking listen to him!" Nathan yelled, bringing her gaze to him.

He was facing off with Julio, who no longer held a gun, but was wielding a knife instead. The man was deadly with a weapon, moving it back and forth expertly in front of Nathan. Fear filled Harper when she saw the number of small gashes he'd already scored on the man she loved.

"How many more are out there?" Chance demanded, kneeling beside Harper, his gun held out in front of him. When there was no response, he growled, "Kid, how many more of these assholes are with you?"

Trey raised his head, his entire body shaking as he replied, "Two. One was in the barn. The other one went in the house from the back door."

"Make that one," a female voice said, as the screen door was shoved open and a man pushed roughly to the porch, landing beside Harper, his hands tightly cuffed behind him.

"Katy," Harper gasped, never so grateful to see someone in her life. "You're here."

"Creed has the guy in the barn. Sorry, we showed up late, Harper. By the time we got news that these hooligans had rolled through town, they were already here. You almost had all the fun without us."

"You call this fun?" Chance asked, his gaze dropping to his shoulder again.

"Obviously, you need to react faster," Katy quipped, sending him a saucy smile before glancing over at Nathan. "Looks like your man is getting a little pissed, Harper."

Harper looked over at Nathan, holding her breath as Julio feigned to the left, and lunged toward Nathan with the knife again.

"Fuck this shit," Nathan snarled, as the knife nicked him. Pulling back his fist, he let if fly, grunting in satisfaction when Julio's head flung back. Julio dropped the knife and slowly fell to the ground. Kicking the knife out of the way, Nathan caught a pair of handcuffs Rayna threw his way and slapped them on Julio. "He's all yours," he told Creed, turning toward Harper.

"What? I thought being the FBI, you would want to handle this?"

"I'm retired."

Hope began to fill Harper, and she slowly moved from Trey, rising to her feet and making her way to the front of the steps. "You mean it? You really are quitting?"

"Harper, girl, I never say anything I don't mean."

Harper cleared the steps and ran to him, sliding her hands around his waist and hugging him close. "I love you, Nathan Brentworth. With all that I am."

Nathan groaned, slowly disengaging her arms from him. "Maybe we better wait for this part until after we take a trip into town." When she looked at him in confusion, he glanced down at himself, a boyish grin crossing his face. "I think I might have overdone it again."

Harper's eyes narrowed on the blood seeping from his wounds, and she shook her head. "It's a good thing you have me to look after you now, Nate."

"Yes," he grinned, his lips covering hers lightly, "it is."

CHAPTER 16

*H*arper knocked on the door, lightly at first, and then louder when there was no answer. She could hear someone on the other side, and then it swung open and a beautiful young woman with long, straight brown hair and large brown eyes full of wonder appeared. "Harper? What are you doing here?" Her gaze went past her to the man who stood next to her, and she asked, "Who are you?"

There was no fear in her voice, only curiosity. Rosa Jarez had come a long way in the past twelve years. She was a strong woman, married to a man who loved her above all else, and they had three beautiful children together. Harper was proud of the person she'd become, and thanked God every day that she had been a part of helping her survive the trials and tribulations she'd been through to get where she was today.

"Rosa, this is Nathan. He's...well," for the first time in a long time, Harper was at a loss for words. How did she describe the man standing next to her?

"I'm Nathan Brentworth, ma'am," Nathan said, slipping an arm around Harper's waist. "I've heard several wonderful things about you. It's nice to finally meet you."

A beautiful smile graced Rosa's face, lighting up her dark eyes. "It's nice to meet you, too, Mr. Brentworth. Won't you both come in?"

"Rosa. Who's here?"

Rosa's husband, Matthew, appeared beside her, opening the door wider as he smiled at Harper. "It's nice to see you again, Harper. I didn't know you were coming for a visit."

"Actually," Harper said gently, her eyes on Rosa, "we've come with news."

"Yes?"

"Rosa," a voice said tentatively from behind Nathan and Harper. "Is that really you?"

Rosa's eyes widened, and she pulled away from her husband and rushed through the door. "Mama! Oh, Mama!" she cried, moving quickly down the front steps to engulf her mother in a hug. "Mama, I can't believe you're here!"

Harper's heart filled with joy as she watched mother and daughter hold each other for the first time in years. They had both been through so much, they deserved all of the happiness they were about to receive.

"Harper, how is she here?" Rosa rasped, looking over at Harper, fear in her voice. "What if Julio finds out? What if he hurts her?"

"Julio is in prison," Harper interrupted, pulling away from Nathan to walk down the stairs and rest a hand gently on Rosa's arm. "He has many deaths on his hands, Rosa. He won't ever be getting out. His gang has dissolved, many of them in prison now as well. It's safe for your mother to be here. Safe for you to live your life without fear."

"You did this," Rosa whispered, tears streaming down her face. "This is because of you, isn't it? You saved me so long ago, and you saved me again now." Huge sobs racked her body as she turned and hugged her mom tightly to her again. "Oh, Mama, I've missed you so much."

"I've missed you too, baby," her mother said through her own tears. "I'm so sorry I didn't know what was going on back then. If only I'd known."

"There wasn't anything you could have done," Rosa said, burying her face in her mother's neck as she cried. "They would have killed you. I'm just so glad you are here now."

"Me, too, baby. Me, too."

Harper felt Nathan before he slipped an arm around her waist from behind, and she leaned back against him. "You are the most amazing woman I have ever met," he said quietly, for her ears alone.

Tilting her head back, Harper smiled and shrugged. "I'm just me."

Nathan chuckled, leaning down to kiss her softly. "I love everything about you."

CHAPTER 17

a week later, Harper stood next to Whisper in the corral by the barn, watching as Sheriff Creed Caldwell's truck came slowly down her drive. Nathan drew her attention as he stepped out of the house, a cup of coffee in his hand. Grinning, she gave Whisper one last pat on her flank and made her way out of the corral and across the lawn to meet Nathan at the foot of the stairs.

"You ready for this?" Nathan asked, an eyebrow raised.

"Always," she told him, relieving him of his cup to take a sip of the coffee.

Creed came to a stop near them and shut off the truck, exiting the vehicle. The passenger door opened slowly, and Trey Richards slid out, nervousness stamped on his face.

"Creed," Nathan said, nodding to him. "Trey."

"Hi, Nathan," Creed replied, grabbing a duffle bag from the back of the truck and bringing it over to drop at Trey's feet "Remember what I told you, boy," he said gruffly. "You've been given a second chance. It's time you turn your life around. Start making better choices. You aren't alone anymore. You have Nathan and Harper, and you have me. If you need anything, anything at all, you call me."

"Yes, sir," Trey whispered, staring at the man in awe. "Thank you," he stuttered.

Creed tilted his Stetson at the boy, waved to Nathan and Harper, and left, leaving Trey trembling in front of the couple.

"Trey," Harper said softly, handing the coffee back to Nathan and stepping closer to the boy. "Do you understand what this place is? What we do here?"

Trey nodded his head slowly, his eyes filling with tears as he rasped, "The sheriff explained it. You're my last chance. I go to prison if I mess up here."

"No, Trey," Harper murmured, smiling gently at him. "Sheriff Caldwell said we are your second chance. Not your last chance. I don't believe in last chances."

"You don't?" Trey's eyes began to fill with hope as he watched her closely.

"No, I don't. Sometimes, we all need more than one chance. Sometimes, we need two, three, or four, or even more. None of us is perfect. All we can do is try our hardest to be the best person we can be."

"Why are you doing this for me?" Trey asked, his gaze dropping to his feet. "I tried to kill you."

"No, Trey, you never would have hurt me. I know that, and so do you."

Trey lifted bright blue eyes wet with tears to look at her. "What happens now?"

"Now, you get the chance at life you were never given before," Nathan said, walking over to pick up his bag. "You get a place to live, food to eat, and the chance to learn to become a responsible adult. And you know what the best part is, son?" When Trey shook his head, his lips trembling, Nathan reached out and squeezed his shoulder gently. "You get this wonderful woman on your side. She will care for you, she will fight for you, she will stand behind you no matter what."

"I don't know what to say," Trey whispered.

"You don't have to say anything," Harper told him, waving her hand to Nickolas, who was walking their way. "Nickolas, I've put Trey in your cabin. Can you help him out, please? Show him the ropes?"

"Sure," Nickolas said, closing the distance between them and taking Trey's bag from Nathan. "Come on, man. You can have the bunk above mine. Unless you don't like heights? I'll switch ya if you need me to."

Trey's gaze swung from Harper to Nickolas, and he asked, "Why are you being so nice to me? We hurt you. Beat you."

"No," Nickolas said, shaking his head. "The other jerks hurt me. You never laid a hand on me. You slipped me food when they weren't watching. You tried to get them to stop."

"It was wrong," Trey whispered. "I didn't want any part of it."

"Hey, man. I know what it's like to be forced to do stuff you don't want to do," Nickolas said. "It sucks, but you don't have a choice. You do what you have to do to survive."

"Yeah."

"Well, we got a chance to be who we want to be here. Not who others want us to be."

Trey nodded, his eyes full of wonder as he looked around the ranch. "I can't believe it."

"I couldn't either at first," Nickolas admitted, "but this place is the real deal, and so is Harper. Come on, let's get you situated; and then I'll show you around the place. We all have chores we have to do. I'm not sure what yours will be, but I'll show you what I do."

Harper watched them leave, a smile on her lips. Trey was going to be just fine, but she was worried about Nickolas.

"Nathan, are you any closer to finding out who wants to take Nickolas from us?"

"No," he said quietly, "but my contacts in the bureau are working on it."

"How do we protect him?"

"The only way we can," Nathan said, slipping an arm around her waist. "Together."

"When do you go back to Virginia?" Harper asked as she slipped into bed beside Nathan that night.

"Actually, I wanted to talk to you about that."

Harper froze, worried that maybe Nathan had decided to stay with the FBI. He'd never given any indication that he might leave. He'd even been staying in her room every night, although they kept his things in the spare bedroom so they didn't attract the children's attention.

When she didn't respond, he pulled her close as he promised, "If you don't like what I have to say, then I will retire fully. You are my everything now, Harper. All that I need."

Harper sighed, knowing she was being unreasonable. It was wrong for her to put him in a position where he had to choose between her and his work. "I love you, Nate. That isn't going to change, even if you are gone for months at a time. I want you to be happy, and if your undercover missions make you happy, then continue doing them. I'll be here waiting when you get home."

"Ah, sweetheart," Nathan said, sliding a hand up under the long nightshirt she wore to gently cup her breast. "I'm not going undercover again. You are all the excitement this old man needs." Bending his head, he lightly bit her nipple through her shirt, chuckling when she jumped. "The Bureau has asked me to start training new agents part time in Dallas."

"Part time?"

"Yes. They have enough full-time instructors, but no one to fill in when needed." Nipping at her other nipple through the shirt, he asked, "What do you think?"

"Yes," she gasped, pushing into him.

"Yes?"

"Oh, yes," she cried, shuddering when he slipped his hand down her waist, over her stomach, and cupped her mound, sliding a finger deep inside. "Nate, please!"

"Please what?" he teased, sliding his finger in and out of her, and then adding another as he began to rub his cock against her.

"Nate!"

"Tell me what you need," he demanded, capturing her nipple through the shirt and sucking.

"Oh, God!" Shoving hard at his shoulders, she pushed him over, knowing he let her. Rising on her knees, she slid over him, grateful she'd started sleeping without her panties and that her man slept in the nude. Reaching down, she held his cock still and slid down over it, moaning as his thickness filled her. She would never get tired of the way it felt when he made love to her.

"Harper." Nathan groaned her name, grasping her hips as she began to move. "I love the way you feel, woman."

"Yes!"

It was as if they'd always been together. They belonged together. He fit her perfectly; like he was made for her.

Nathan let her have control for a moment, but then he took over, holding her still as he slammed into her again and again. Harper felt the pressure building inside of her, and then she went over the edge, screaming his name as she came, Nathan following right behind.

She lay in his arms later, gently tracing small patterns on his chest. "Nathan, I just want you to know how much it means to me that you are going to move here from your home. I would move wherever you wanted me to, but I would worry about the children."

Nathan placed a finger on her lips to stop her from continuing. Cupping her cheek, he lifted her face to look at him. "Before I met you, I had no real home. I lived wherever the job took me. You are my home, Harper Daley. Not a place, a person. You."

"Oh, Nathan."

"I've never loved anyone else the way that I love you."

Snuggling close to him, Harper smiled through her tears. "I love you, too, Nathan."

Make sure and visit my website for information on all of my books, and to sign up for my Newsletter where you will receive all of the latest information on new releases, sales, and more!

Website: **http://www.dawnsullivanauthor.com/**

I would love to have you join my reader's group, Author Dawn Sullivan's RARE Rebels, so that we can hang out and chat, and where you will also get sneak peeks of cover reveals, read excerpts before anyone else, and more!

https://www.facebook.com/groups/AuthorDawnSullivansRebelReaders/

Dawn Sullivan

ABOUT THE AUTHOR

Dawn Sullivan has a wonderful, supportive husband, and three beautiful children. She enjoys spending time with them, which normally involves some baseball, shooting hoops, taking walks, watching movies, and reading.

Her passion for reading began at a very young age and only grew over time. Whether she was bringing home a book from the library or sneaking one of her mother's romance novels to read by the light in the hallway when she was supposed to be sleeping, Dawn always had a book. She reads several different genres and subgenres, but Paranormal Romance and Romantic Suspense are her favorites.

Dawn has always made up stories of her own, and finally decided to start sharing them with others. She hopes everyone enjoys reading them as much as she enjoys writing them.

facebook.com/dawnsullivanauthor

twitter.com/dawn_author

instagram.com/dawn_sullivan_author

Made in the USA
Coppell, TX
16 March 2023